NOT THE WORST FRIEND IN THE WORLD

by Anne Rellihan

HOLIDAY HOUSE · NEW YORK

HOLIDAY HOUSE is registered in the U.S. Patent and Trademark Office.

Printed and bound in December 2023 at Maple Press, York, PA, USA.

www.holidayhouse.com

First Edition

1 3 5 7 9 10 8 6 4 2

Library of Congress Cataloging-in-Publication Data is available.

ISBN: 978-0-8234-5479-2 (hardcover)

For Will, Jack, Claire, and Kate

Cece Clark-Duncan passed me a note on the thirty-fourth day of sixth grade.

If she had passed it twenty-five days earlier, I might have ignored it. Or worse, showed it to Francie.

At first, I didn't believe the note was meant for me. Yet there was my name, plain as day, carefully written across the front in bubbly print—*Louise*. She'd even put a heart above the *i*.

My name *is* Louise Bennett, but the fact that she'd written "Louise" revealed her newness. Only teachers and my grandmother call me Louise. Everyone else calls me Lou. Francie shortened it the day I met her in kindergarten. She said Louise sounded like a grandma name, so she made it better. I liked Lou more, too. Louise held on to her mom's leg at the playground because she was scared of the slides and the big kids. Lou was brave and smart and funny. She had to be. Francie Fitzpatrick was her best friend.

Emphasis on *was*. Past tense. Because then sixth grade happened. And Tommy Maguire happened. And the dumb fight happened. And just like that, I became invisible.

So there I was, trying to pretend I didn't care about any of it, when I got a note from the only sixth grader who was a bigger outsider than me.

It happened during our first geography quiz of the year. The end of September and it was still blazing hot in Mayfield, Missouri. I sat at my desk sweating through my white uniform shirt. Sweat pooled under my arms and my legs stuck together underneath my plaid skirt. My dark hair hung in clumps on my neck and frizzed around my freckled face. But being invisible made it easier to forget the frizz and focus on my plan.

My plan had one step.

Step 1: Get Francie to talk to me.

It was written on a clean page of my leather-bound note-book. I had underlined Step 1 about a million times, drew doodles all around it, but was no closer to accomplishing it. A plan isn't much of a plan with only one step. I was stuck remembering those text messages and hearing myself say the terrible, horrible things I couldn't unsay over and over again. It had been more than three weeks, and that day kept replaying in my mind like a movie. I about threw up every time I watched it.

I didn't blame anyone for hating me. If I'm being honest, I hated me, too.

"Alright kiddos, please clear your desks. All you need is a pencil and your bright minds," Mrs. Jackson said in her singsong voice, the one she used when she wanted to make something boring sound fun. She held a stack of geography quizzes.

"C'mon Mrs. J! School just started," Tommy Maguire called from the back of the room.

"We've been in school over a month now, Tommy, which is why you should know to study when I say there will be a quiz and to raise your hand if you want to speak." No more singsong.

Two rows ahead, Francie's hand shot into the air.

"Yes, Francie?" Mrs. Jackson said.

"Can we at least make it open note? I've been super busy after school lately." Francie turned and smiled at Tommy. My stomach rolled.

"Nice try, Francie. Clear your desk."

A few kids grumbled.

"Louise, I asked you to clear your desk. It's quiz time," Mrs. Jackson said.

My head resting on my arm, I traced Francie's name in my notebook over and over. I shoved the notebook into my bag just in time to see Francie mouth something to Tommy. He smirked. She giggled. I laid my head back on my arm.

That's when I saw the note. Someone had slid it from the row behind me and it had landed under my desk. I was about to kick it into the aisle so its real owner could grab it when I saw the bubbly print. *Louise.*

It had to be a joke. I was certain if I picked it up, the empty quiz air would fill with muffled laughter. I scanned the row behind me. All sets of eyes were fixed on their quizzes. Except one. Cece Clark-Duncan's round brown eyes stared right at me. She nodded toward the note, so I reached my hand down, swept it up, and slid it under the quiz on my desk.

No one laughed. No one moved. I glanced back at Cece, who moved her pencil furiously across the page. She pushed a piece of loose red hair back toward her messy ponytail.

Cece was brand-new at Our Lady of Perpetual Help. The two of us were tied for Sixth Grader You Didn't Want to Be. I figured she didn't know offering me, of all people, a gesture of friendship was a dumb move on her part. That was before I knew the note wasn't exactly a gesture of friendship.

Cece's note was folded into an origami frog. Francie's notes to me had always been carefully folded, too. Hearts, stars, arrows. The frog made me think Cece was the type of girl who had passed lots of notes in her life before Mayfield.

I pulled the tongue of the frog, and the note opened.

I have a problem…a pretty big one. Can you help? If the answer is yes, meet me after school. If it's no, rip this up and pretend I never sent it. —CCD

2

I read and reread Cece's note about a million times. I stared at it until the words blurred together.

I thought of everything I knew about Cece. If I'm being honest, it wasn't much.

Cece had arrived in Mayfield two weeks ago with her dad and a black-and-white cat. I saw them from the curb outside the Riverport Market the day they pulled up in a U-Haul. They moved into the empty apartment above the Able & Payne Law Offices, catty-corner from the Market on First Street. My mom is the administrative assistant at Able & Payne, so she's the one who told me they were moving in.

The Clark-Duncans' arrival was the most interesting thing to happen in Mayfield since our third-grade teacher, Sister Genevieve, packed her Yorkie and moved to Florida with a man she'd met online. I guess she didn't think her sacred nun vows were all that sacred. Investigating the

Clark-Duncans was exactly the type of thing Francie and I would have done together, back before I said the terrible, horrible things and ruined our friendship. But when Cece moved in, it had been exactly one week since Francie had spoken a word to me.

That day, I bought a gumball from the dusty antique machine inside the Riverport Market, plopped onto the curb, and tried not to think about how much more fun this would be with Francie sitting next to me. A girl around my age jumped out of the cab of the truck holding the cat.

I opened my notebook and scribbled my observations.

Redheaded girl. Messy ponytail. 11ish years old.

Tall, skinny man. Dark hair, gray on the sides. Needs to shave. Bags under his eyes.

Man asks girl several questions. No response. Approximately six eye rolls and three heavy sighs.

The redheaded girl turned away from her dad and looked in my direction. She stared at my notebook, and I dropped my pen. We made eye contact. Her stare gave way to a smile, and she waved before following her dad inside.

The door to Able & Payne swung open and Opal Duncan stepped outside. Opal Duncan went to church at Our Lady of Perpetual Help, and I saw her at Mass on Sundays. She was the type of old lady that judged you for breathing wrong. I'd never seen her with other people. I grabbed my pen.

Opal goes in for a hug, redhead shrugs her off

Opal Duncan: redhead's grandmother?

Is that why they're in Mayfield?

I imagined what Francie would say if she were here. The Old Francie would concoct some wild story about what this girl was doing above the law offices and why cranky old Opal Duncan was involved. The New Francie would tell me we were getting too old for games and say there were better ways to spend our time, which meant following Tommy Maguire around. She probably wouldn't have come with me in the first place, but I didn't know that for sure, and sometimes it was easier to remember things the way they had been before Francie changed.

I closed my notebook and waited for them to come back outside. When several minutes passed with no sign of them, I stood, dusted off my faded jean shorts, and headed home.

Cece started at Our Lady of Perpetual Help on the following Monday. Francie, Madison Brewer, and the other girls swarmed her right away. She was a foreign species, and they wanted a closer look. We didn't get many new students. But by the end of the week, they all lost interest. Everyone fell back into their old patterns. Everyone except me—I was invisible.

Now, with Cece's note in my lap, I was glad I was invisible.

I finished my quiz and pulled my notebook out. I positioned the note so Mrs. Jackson couldn't see it, but I could if I tipped back in my chair a little.

I watched Francie finish her quiz. She took out a blue Sharpie and colored her fingernails with it. She held her hand so Madison could see. It gave me that I'm-either-going-to-throw-up-or-cry feeling, so I put my head back on my arm and turned to a clean page in my notebook.

I wrote Cece's name at the top of the page, hoping it would push Francie out of my mind. I searched my brain for a problem that could be big enough, and secret enough, to make Cece write a note like that.

Something to do with her cat? But why is that a secret?

Sad-eyed man: is he sick? In trouble? Dangerous?

Able & Payne: weird place to live ... are they hiding from something? Someone?

Opal Duncan: Holding them hostage?

The questions swirled in my head and onto the page, growing wilder as I went.

"Louise, if you're done, please read a book." Mrs. Jackson's voice broke through as I envisioned Cece's father as a secret agent busting an underground crime ring in Mayfield.

I read back through my notes and scratched them out, ripping the page in two places. I shoved the notebook into my desk.

Maybe my notebook *was* getting weird. Francie had told me as much, and she was the one who'd given me all of my notebooks. Francie and I used to play this spying game. It started in first grade, and then in second grade, I read *Harriet the Spy*, and I decided we needed a notebook so we could write what we saw, like Harriet does. At first, we used a regular spiral notebook. Then on my eighth birthday, Francie presented me with a leather-bound notebook.

"For Mayfield's real-life Harriet the Spy," she had said. She gave me the same leather-bound notebook every year after that.

Up ahead of me, Francie was writing a note. She looked back at Tommy. It was probably for him.

"Francie, you, too. Take out a book, please," Mrs. Jackson said.

"Sure thing, Mrs. J."

She pulled out a book, set it on the corner of her desk, and kept on writing her note.

I pretended to tie my shoe so I could turn around in my chair without Mrs. Jackson noticing. Cece was done with the quiz, too. She held a book, and from the way she stared at the page, I didn't think she was reading it.

I sat up. Francie folded her note into the shape of a heart. Then she took her blue Sharpie and wrote something across the front. I could see a big, bubbly *T* from where I sat.

"Francie, I asked you to read a book," Mrs. Jackson said.

"Okay, I will, but can I get a tissue first? My allergies are literally so bad this time of year." Francie smiled sweetly.

"That's fine, but then I need to see you reading."

Francie walked toward the tissue box sitting on a shelf at the back of the room. As she walked by Tommy's desk, she flipped the heart-shaped note onto it. My stomach dropped to my toes like it had when Francie had convinced me to ride the Screamin' Eagle at Six Flags. I counted backward from thirty. Ever since I'd said the terrible, horrible things, counting backward helped when my breath got stuck and my heart threatened to beat out of my chest. Every time Francie brushed by me without a word or giggled at something dumb Tommy said, I counted backward.

Three. Two. One. Zero. My breathing slowed. I reached for my notebook and tore out a page.

Cece,

Meet me in front of the buses after school.

Lou

The bell rang, and it was like someone had kicked a hornet's nest as everyone leapt out of their chairs and jostled toward the door. Francie looped her arm through Madison Brewer's in a way that was so familiar it made my lip quiver. *Thirty. Twenty-nine. Twenty-eight.*

"Let's ride the bus to my house and then walk to the fields to watch football practice." Francie's voice was low, but I heard anyway.

Francie pulled Madison toward the door. I zipped Cece's note into the front pocket of my backpack and packed and unpacked my math book three times before I finally got up. I poked my head out of the classroom first to make sure Francie was gone. The hallway was empty, and I spotted Cece's red ponytail as she pushed the big double front doors open, so I half jogged to catch her.

By the time I made it outside, Cece was standing in front of the bus line. She paced back and forth with her arms folded across her chest. She uncrossed them when she saw me coming, pulled her ponytail tighter, and gave me a little wave.

My eyes scanned the crowded sidewalk for Francie, and when I didn't see her, I returned Cece's wave.

"Hey," she said. I'd never heard her voice outside of class.

"Hey," I said.

"So, I've been thinking about what I should say to you all afternoon. What do you like to do for fun? Or what'd you think of that geography quiz? But then I figured, what's the point? You already read the note. None of that matters. Right?"

My eyes wandered toward the sidewalk crowd, which had now mostly filtered onto the buses.

"Right," I said. "I mean right, I read the note, but we can talk about the geography quiz if you want."

"I don't want to talk about the geography quiz," Cece said.

"Okay. We can talk about whatever you want."

Cece looked around and lowered her voice. "The truth is I need help. I've needed help since I got here. I didn't know who to ask, until I thought of you."

This shocked me. I'd believed I was invisible.

"I'm not sure how much help I'll be—"

The scenarios I'd scribbled in my notebook turned into headlines that flashed around in my brain: *FBI Uncovers Local Crime Ring. Sick Man Moves to Mayfield to Fulfill Dying Wish. Girl Hidden Away in Small Town Law Office.*

Cece and I were the only kids left on the sidewalk. The bus doors creaked closed, one by one.

"You're smart. Even though you're always writing in that notebook, you still know the answer every time Mrs. Jackson calls on you."

Someone smart would have ditched that dumb notebook the first time Francie said it was weird. Someone smart would never have said the terrible, horrible things I couldn't unsay.

"And you're brave. You're always alone, and it's like you hardly even mind."

Someone brave wouldn't use her bathroom pass to cry in a stall. Someone brave wouldn't count backward in her head all day to keep her heart from exploding.

"I don't think you get it," I said.

"Actually, I think we have a lot in common."

The buses rumbled awake and pulled away from the school, one by one. Cece lifted the flap on her messenger bag and pulled out a notebook with a silver constellation stamped into its black cover. As she pressed it into my hands, a head poked out the windows of Bus 52.

"Oh look. The two freaks found each other. Looks like *Louise* finally has a new friend," Braden Kelly yelled.

As his words poured out and rolled down the street with the bus, the window behind Braden's opened. A white-blonde head I'd know anywhere popped out.

Francie's eyes caught mine for the first time in twenty-four days. They were hard and angry. Behind that, they were hurt.

KINDERGARTEN

I met Francie on the first day of school in Sister Mary Joseph's kindergarten class. Her hair looked like it hadn't been combed that morning, the pleats on her uniform jumper went every which way, and her white polo had a faded stain on the collar.

Sister Mary Joseph had us sit in a circle on a giant, colorful rug. Francie plopped next to me and smiled. She sat with her legs folded criss-cross applesauce, like Sister showed us, and her knee touched mine.

We stared at Sister Mary Joseph, wide-eyed and waiting. "Please share your name and one thing you'd like the class to know about you," Sister said.

When it was my turn, I whispered, "My name is Louise Bennett and I'm going to have a baby brother." Even I barely heard what I said.

"Louder! Speak so Jesus can hear you," Sister Mary Joseph commanded.

"She said her name's Lou and she's gonna have a baby brother," Francie shouted.

Sister nodded. Jesus could hear Francie loud and clear.

Francie was next. "My name's Mary Frances Fitzpatrick, but everyone calls me Francie." Jesus wasn't missing a word. "I've got two sisters. They're both named Mary, too. We have to use our second name or no one would know who's getting in trouble for what. My mama prayed to the Virgin Mary for all girls and that's what happened. So, she named us Mary, because of the holiness. The end. Amen."

When it was time for recess, Francie stood next to me in line. She looped her arm through mine.

"We're playing together," she commanded.

We burst through the recess doors, our arms still looped together. She pulled me to the rusty slide at the back of the playground, and we sat underneath it.

Kindergarten was the best place in the world.

"Let's play a game, Lou," Francie suggested. "My sister Bernie taught it to me. It's called Curse War." Her eyes sparkled. "You start out whispering a curse word. Then it's the other person's turn. You go back and forth saying them a little louder. The person who gets the loudest is the winner."

Francie said word after word I'd never heard before. I stared at her, eyes wide, and repeated after her for two rounds before I got scared. Francie got all the way up to her talking-to-Jesus shout.

And then Sister Mary Joseph stood over us.

"Mary Frances! That is enough! March yourself straight to Dr. Morgan's office."

I froze to the spot. Francie put both hands over her mouth

to trap her giggle and then skipped off toward the recess doors.

Francie was a legend at Our Lady of Perpetual Help. And because she chose me that day, I got to be kind of legendary, too. Francie never told anyone I chickened out after two rounds. It was dumb, but I was glad she kept that secret.

5

Cece and I stood there in a cloud of exhaust. Bus 52 paused at the stop sign at the end of the block and then turned left toward the south side of town, where Francie lived. I squeezed my eyes shut and willed the sidewalk to open and swallow me whole. When that didn't happen, I willed my tears not to spill over and the pounding in my chest to quiet.

"What is wrong with Braden? He is the absolute worst." Cece spat her words and stared at the space where the buses had been with a look so mean it could scare a nun. The way her face scrunched made the freckles threaten to pop right off her pale nose.

"At my old school, they would consider that bullying. He'd never get away with it. What did you do to deserve that?"

I said a silent prayer that Cece wouldn't find out.

"It doesn't matter. That's how Braden is. He's mean for no reason and he's mean to everyone. He's been like that since kindergarten."

I focused my attention back to Cece's notebook. I held it palms up like some kind of awkward offering.

"What is this?" I said, running one hand over the cover.

"It's a notebook."

"I can see that. I meant what's in it? Why'd you give it to me?"

In a million, trillion years I wouldn't hand over my notebook. Not to my mother. Not to Francie. And certainly not to a perfect stranger.

"I told you. I think we have a lot in common. The first thing I noticed about you was that notebook. I saw it the day we moved in. And you never stop writing in it at school. Haven't you noticed me writing, too?"

"No," I admitted.

"It doesn't matter. I noticed yours. Have you read *Harriet the Spy*?"

"Yes!" I said. "That's where we got the idea for the notebook in the first place."

"We?"

"I meant me. That's where I got the idea." I wasn't ready to talk about Francie, or our game, or why I was invisible.

"Me too. My mom read the book to me a few years ago. It was one of her favorites when she was a kid." Cece tightened her ponytail again and looked away from me. It was like she was searching the clouds for something.

After a few seconds, she turned back.

"But I don't spy on people like Harriet did. I mostly write things that I don't want other people to know. What about you? Do you spy on people? Is that what you were doing the day we moved in?"

Heat rose in my cheeks. That's *exactly* what I'd been doing. Or trying to do.

"No," I lied. "I used to investigate stuff. But not anymore. Now I mostly do what you do—write the things I don't want other people to know. I was there that day because my mom works at Able & Payne. She told me there was someone my age moving in. I was going to say hi, but I never got the chance."

"Oh." Cece's face fell a little, like that wasn't the answer she was looking for. "I don't think spying is weird, if that's what you think. In fact, it's kind of the reason I was drawn to you in the first place. It was like the universe was trying to tell me something."

"Tell you what?"

"That you could help." She lowered her voice again and shifted her eyes from the school to where the buses had been and then back to me.

"What does your notebook have to do with it? Do you want me to read what's in it?" I asked.

There was a rushing in my ears, like the river after it rains, just thinking about someone reading my notebook. What if someone saw the full-page list I'd written the night before: *Reasons Why I Hate the New Francie*. It made me think of the part in *Harriet the Spy* when Harriet's classmates read her notebook. Nothing could be worse.

Cece grabbed the notebook back. "Geez, would you let someone you hardly know read your entire notebook?"

"God, no. But I wouldn't just hand it over to someone either."

"I only wanted you to see it." Cece shoved her notebook

back into her bag and pulled out a file folder, the kind teachers use to hand back tests so no one else can see your grade. "Here. Take this."

She pressed the folder into my hands, the same way she'd given me the notebook.

"What is it?"

"A page from my notebook, and one other thing. Hopefully it will help you understand why I need you."

Our eyes met. It was like she wanted to tell me a million things without saying anything at all.

"Just read what's in there," she pleaded.

She turned then and walked down the sidewalk toward First Street, and her apartment. She was almost to the crosswalk when she spun around to face me.

"Oh, and Lou?"

"Yeah?"

"Please, please, please don't show anyone."

"I won't," I promised, placing my right hand over my heart.

The river sound whirred through my ears again. I clutched the folder to my chest, and I said one more prayer. I prayed Cece wouldn't find out what Francie already knew.

I'm not the kind of friend you should trust with your secrets.

6

I kept the folder clutched to my chest the entire walk home. My house was only eight blocks from school, but ever since I said the terrible, horrible things, I took the long way.

The straight shot from Our Lady of Perpetual Help to my house led me right past the fields at Mayfield Municipal Park, where the sixth-grade boys practiced football. It was also where Francie planted herself every afternoon. Like hooting and hollering while the boys clobbered each other was her afterschool job.

I had a list in my notebook: *Good Things About Francie Hating Me. 1. Not watching dumb boys practice dumb football.*

My new route swung me out past River Bend Estates, which sounded fancy, but was a trailer park. Clinton Mulvaney lived there. His hair and skin were all one color—the same beige-ish as the walls at Our Lady of Perpetual Help. He blended in. No one paid attention to him. But no one bothered him either.

At our school, everyone played the same role they'd played since kindergarten. It was comfortable that way. But now everything was shifting, and I couldn't stop it. My fight with Francie had turned me into a Clinton Mulvaney.

The new route added at least ten minutes to my walk. I tried distracting myself to keep from opening the folder. But when I didn't think about what might be inside, I saw Francie's eyes instead. They were lined with mascara so thick it turned her eyelashes into spider legs. The makeup was part of Francie's new sixth-grade look. It was also on my *Good Things About Francie Hating Me* list. 4. *Francie can't talk me into wearing mascara (looks painful)*.

The expression in her eyes today was new, too. But there was no list for that. That part was my fault.

A block from home, I took off in a sprint. Maybe if I ran fast enough, I'd leave Francie's eyes behind on the sidewalk.

"LouLou!" My brother, Tripp, sat on the concrete step in front of our house. He was surrounded by about a bajillion stuffed animals. He held his favorite, a princess doll he called Lady Rainbow the Magnificent, on his lap.

Our house was a perfectly symmetrical white rectangle—one nine-paned window on either side of the yellow front door. It looked exactly like the house next door, and the house next door to that, and the house next door to that. The yellow door was the only difference. We'd gotten used to giving our address that way: "726 Commerce Street—the one with the yellow door."

"Do you want to play Secret Kingdom? Lady Rainbow has to save the castle from the wildebeests," Tripp said. He held a stuffed bear, an Elmo, and a ragged-looking bunny.

"Not today, buddy. I've got a lot of homework," I lied, stepping over his entourage on my way to the door.

Mom bustled around the kitchen with my baby sister, Orla, on her hip.

"Lou! I'm so glad you're home, honey girl. Here. Can you take the baby for a sec?" She held Orla out to me. Orla's chubby legs kicked in the air. I set Cece's folder on the table and grabbed my sister.

Mom pulled random things from the cabinet and filled a paper grocery bag with them.

"Remember, sweetness, I'm going to Katy's tonight for a girls' night? Clear my head a little from the chaos around here?"

She gestured toward Orla. Orla screeched like she knew Mom was talking about her.

"I told Katy I'd come by early to help. James has the dinner shift tonight."

James is my stepdad, and Tripp and Orla's dad. My dad lives two hours away in Kansas City. He and Mom split up when I was two. He drives a truck, so he isn't home that much. I see him for a week during Christmas break, two weeks during the summer, and some random weekends in between.

Having part of me in two places is hard sometimes, but I'm used to it. Or at least I was. Things with my dad had changed over the last year. Somehow, fifth grade ended and everything got mixed up and backward. With everyone. Even Mom seemed different. She was extra stressed with work and my siblings, and she'd been having a lot of girls' nights.

"I forgot you were going out tonight," I said. "I have homework. I can't watch Tripp and Orla."

"Honey, please? James will be at work until late, and I'd ask Mrs. Barnes but I asked her for a favor with the kids earlier this week."

James works in the kitchen at Riverfront Bistro, the fanciest restaurant in Mayfield. He's going to open his own restaurant someday.

Mom gave me a pleading look.

"Mom—"

"You could see if Francie wants to come help. She loves playing with the baby."

"She's got homework, too." I hadn't told Mom about Francie yet, and she'd been too busy to notice.

"I'll put a movie on. You can put Orla in the playpen. Nannie is going to come by after she gets off work to put Orla to bed." Our grandma was around so much, she was almost like another parent.

It was pointless to keep arguing. Soon, her pleading look would become her you're-going-to-do-it-because-I-said-so look.

"Okay, fine. But you owe me."

Mom hugged me and kissed my forehead. "Thank you, and yes, I owe you, times a million." I pushed her away, but only half seriously.

Once Mom left, I settled Tripp and Orla with a movie and tried to look at Cece's folder. Except Tripp still wanted to play Secret Kingdom and shoved a new animal in my face every two seconds, and Orla hated being in her playpen and screamed until I picked her up. I got the folder out with her on my lap, but when she gummed one of the corners, I took the folder to my room and set it on my desk. I went back to the living room and waited for Nannie.

Tap. Tap. Tappity Tap. Our special knock.

"Yoo-hoo! Where are my honey bugs? Nannie's here," Nannie said when I opened the front door.

I shoved Orla at her. "Hi," I said. "I think she needs a diaper change." I turned on my heels and headed for my room.

"My, my, I'm delighted to see you, too, Louise," Nannie said, snuggling Orla into her soft chest.

"Sorry, Nannie. I have a ton of homework." I didn't turn around. I knew Nannie's feelings weren't hurt. She was already busy cooing and making googly eyes at Orla.

Once I closed my bedroom door, I grabbed Cece's folder and sat on my bed with my knees tucked beneath me. I smoothed the tangled, faded comforter. I took a deep breath. Cece had handed me the folder herself, but I felt like I was doing something wrong, like I was about to read something I shouldn't.

I opened the folder. Staring back at me was a page that could've been ripped out of my own notebook. It was a list. Penned across the top in Cece's loopy handwriting:

Reasons I Think I Was Kidnapped

I blinked a few times to make sure I'd read it right. But there it was plain as day.

Reasons I Think I Was Kidnapped

1. Parents can't take a kid somewhere without telling the other parent.

2. If my dad told my mom, there's no way she would've let me go.

3. My mom was coming home.

4. My mom loves me.

My heart beat out of control. I counted backward—*thirty, twenty-nine, twenty-eight*. I got to sixteen before my hand stopped shaking enough to turn the page.

Behind the list was a printout from a legal website.

PARENTAL KIDNAPPING

Parental Kidnapping is defined as the concealment, taking, or retention of a child by one parent in violation of the rights of the other parent. Sadly, thousands of children are kidnapped by a parent every year in the United States. Make no mistake, parental kidnapping is illegal.

Concealment. Kidnapped. Illegal. These words joined the jumble in my head. That day outside the Riverport Market. The sad-eyed man. The U-Haul. Opal Duncan. What had I missed? I'd been so consumed by missing Francie that the details of that day blurred together. I wracked my brain for something, *anything*, that would make what Cece wrote make sense. Instead, the river whirred through my ears and my heart threatened to jump right out of my chest.

I turned back to Cece's list.

4. My mom loves me.

Fifteen. Fourteen. Thirteen.

Cece's folder was a magnet. I couldn't pull myself away. After I read it about a million times, I buried it in my pajama drawer. That lasted about thirty seconds before I got it out again.

I wanted to tell Mom, but this wasn't my secret to tell. At least not yet, not before I talked to Cece.

I slept with the folder under my pillow.

My dreams slipped through my fingers when I tried pulling them into focus, but I knew the sad-eyed man and Opal Duncan were with me all night.

In the morning, I decided packing the folder in my backpack was better than leaving it in my room.

"Honey girl, are you up? If you don't leave now, you're going to be late," Mom called to me from the kitchen, where she was getting Tripp and Orla ready for daycare.

I knew I would be late. I wanted to be late. Between Francie's face in the bus window and Cece's folder, I didn't want to step foot inside Our Lady of Perpetual Help a minute before Mrs. Jackson told everyone to find their seats.

"I overslept," I responded from behind my closed bedroom door. "Can you drop me off today?"

That guaranteed a tardy slip.

Mom spent fifteen minutes trying to convince Tripp he didn't need to wear four shirts to daycare, she cursed under her breath as she wrangled Orla into her car seat, and she made two trips back inside the house for Orla's bottle and Tripp's Lady Rainbow.

I walked into the classroom as Dr. Morgan finished the morning prayer over the loudspeaker. Thank goodness. No avoiding eye contact with Francie.

Or figuring out what to say to Cece.

I had no clue how to help her. Her problem was the ocean, and I was a teeny-tiny fish. A teeny-tiny fish who could never figure out what direction to swim.

As I slipped into my seat, I felt Cece's round eyes on me. I didn't dare turn around. Instead I set my notebook on my desk and resumed my usual position. Head on arm. Counting backward until my heart slowed.

I opened my notebook and wrote on a clean page.

Reasons Not to Help Cece

1. Cece's dad could be dangerous or crazy.

2. Cece could be dangerous or crazy.

3. I am not the kind of friend she wants to have.

"Alright, boys and girls. We are starting our day in an exciting way." Mrs. Jackson was singsong.

I wracked my brain trying to remember if we had another quiz.

"I know you're going to love it," she continued.

"Doubt it!" Tommy Maguire yelled from the back. Right on cue, Braden burst out laughing and slapped his desk. Francie laughed loudly, too.

"The grace period on unraised hands is over, Tommy. That's a demerit." She opened her binder and made a mark. "Despite Mr. Maguire's lack of enthusiasm, we are starting the Christ Is Alive! essay contest this week. You may have a sibling or friend who's completed one in the past, and I'm sure they told you how much they loved it. I've even had former students describe it as life-changing."

Mrs. Jackson paused for our reactions.

Tommy stretched and yawned. Francie sighed dramatically. I laid my head back on my arm.

Mrs. Jackson went on, unfazed. "You and a partner will work together to identify a member of our community who leads an exemplary life—showing that Christ is alive and well in Mayfield."

Braden snorted, but Mrs. Jackson continued.

"You'll interview the individual and write an essay. A team of judges will vote, and the most exemplary candidates will be presented at a school-wide assembly at the end of the quarter."

Madison raised her hand.

"Yes, Madison?"

"Do we get to pick our own partner?" she asked, glancing at Francie.

I hoped beyond hope that these would be teacher-assigned pairs. Or better yet, that I could work alone.

"I want both people in the pair to be excited about the

project and in agreement on whom to interview, so, yes, you are trusted to pick your own partner."

A string of "yesses" zipped around the room. Madison pointed at Francie and then at herself. Francie scanned the room before nodding her head. I imagined scrunching myself into a ball and rolling right out of the classroom.

"Go ahead and pair up. Find a spot in the room to sit together, and we'll begin an initial brainstorm," Mrs. Jackson said.

The classroom jostled awake. Chairs shuffled, and everyone called out, staking their claim, making sure they were securely paired before Mrs. Jackson said, "Okay, does everyone have a partner?"

We'd been picking partners since kindergarten, so the pairs were predictable. Tommy and Braden. Annabelle Murphy and Miranda Salinas. Edwin Roper and Peter Kincaid. The list went on. But now, instead of Francie and Lou, it was Francie and Madison.

I stayed glued to my chair, praying that by some miracle, Mrs. Jackson would let me work alone.

Francie watched me. Our eyes met for a split second, and then she turned back to Madison.

"We have an even number, so there should be—" Now Mrs. Jackson was the one watching me.

Braden smiled like he'd solved a complicated math problem. "The new girl doesn't have a partner, Mrs. J. I'm sure Lou would love to work with her. They're friends now, you know, so it all works out." Madison hid a giggle behind her hand.

Twenty-six. Twenty-five. Twenty-four.

Mrs. Jackson turned from me to Cece, expectantly.

I looked at Cece for the first time since yesterday in front of the school. She shrugged. I nodded.

"Perfect," said Mrs. Jackson. "We're all set."

I had no idea what I would say once Mrs. Jackson set us free to work. I couldn't help Cece. There was no way.

Mrs. Jackson handed out instructions while she rambled about how much we would love this project. There were stifled yawns and muffled conversations.

"Judging by the chatter in the room, I can tell you're eager to get started. Let's go over the directions first, and then you'll have time to work together. Francie, can you read the paragraph at the top of the page, please?"

Francie was busy whispering to Madison. She froze, and her face turned red.

"I wasn't raising my hand," she said.

"You and Miss Brewer seem distracted. Can you help us focus back on the directions?"

Francie didn't move. Her face turned a shade brighter. The silence in the room threatened to swallow me whole.

Mrs. Jackson tapped her foot impatiently. "Francie. The paragraph at the top."

Braden elbowed Tommy. They both stared at Francie. Braden had a dumb smirk on this face, like he was about to burst out laughing.

Finally, Francie read. Slowly and deliberately. "There. Are. So. Many." Before she got to the fifth word, she kicked Madison under the desk and coughed a bunch of times like she had something caught in her throat.

Mrs. Jackson was as flustered as I'd ever seen her, like she'd realized her terrible mistake calling on Francie.

Through her sudden coughing attack, Francie managed to say, "I think Madison better read the rest for me. My allergies are out of control."

Madison snapped to attention, like a dog with a treat dangled in front of it.

"I'd love to read the rest," she said.

Gratitude spread across Francie's face, and a pit grew in my stomach. Francie coughed a few more times.

"I could use some water. Is that okay, Mrs. Jackson?" she said.

"Yes, but be quick," Mrs. Jackson said. "Madison, go ahead and read the paragraph, please."

"Thank God," Braden yelled from his seat in the back. "Otherwise we would've been here all day."

He elbowed Tommy again, waiting for a reaction. Tommy looked away, but there were a few giggles around the room. The pit in my stomach turned into a bowling ball.

"Braden, that's enough." Mrs. Jackson's eyes said *don't you dare say another word.*

Francie was at the front of the classroom. She spun around, arms crossed.

"At least I don't have body odor. It's called deodorant, Braden." This time the class didn't contain their laughter. It filled the whole room, and Tommy laughed the loudest.

"Class, I said that is *enough.* Your next stop will be Dr. Morgan's office, where you can explain to her how it is you've spent six years in her *Catholic* school and you still haven't learned the meaning of the word *kindness.*" Mrs. Jackson's face was redder than Francie's. "Francie, get your drink. Braden, keep your comments to yourself. And

Madison, please continue reading the directions for our Christ Is Alive! essay."

Right before she walked out the door, Francie turned and looked at me. Our eyes met for a second. Her jaw clenched. Her eyes filled. Her fists balled. She was as angry as I'd ever seen her.

The noise in my head blared like a car alarm. My heart ached, and counting backward didn't help. I wanted to run out of the room after Francie. I wanted to help her like she would've helped me. I wanted to tell her that Braden was an idiot, and everyone knew it.

I wanted to fill the enormous canyon between us.

But it was too late. So instead, I did the next best thing.

Without giving myself time to change my mind, I ripped the corner off the direction sheet.

I'm ready to help. Let's start right away. Lou

I slid the note over to Cece. A smile snuck across her face. My heart went from a full sprint to a slow jog.

But I still had the bowling ball in my stomach.

~

The next chance Cece and I got to talk was in the cafeteria. It was the first time in twenty-five days that someone had spoken to me at lunch.

The cafeteria doubled as the gym. During lunch, they cranked the basketball hoops up to the ceiling and unfolded long tables with benches attached. There was a table assigned to the sixth-grade girls and one assigned to the sixth-grade boys. Francie chose the seat closest to the boys' table, and Tommy sat right across the aisle from her.

On days one through eight of sixth grade, I'd sat right

next to Francie. Now Madison sat there, proud as could be. I wanted to wipe the smug smile right off her face. But today, I had Cece. I walked into the cafeteria and didn't immediately count backward.

I sat at the end of the table opposite Francie and Madison. The other girls scrunched their bodies toward Francie, like I had a gross disease they were afraid of catching. Cece plunked her tray down across from mine. She pushed her green beans around with her plastic spork.

Finally, she looked up. She spoke in a whisper. "I know you probably think I'm crazy or lying or something."

The words caught in my throat before I could get them out.

"But I'm not. If you knew my mom, you'd know..." Cece's voice broke. Her big, brown eyes filled with tears.

"I don't think you're crazy. Or lying. Not at all. I said I want to help, and I meant it. I'm not sure how, but I read what was in the folder, and——"

"Okay, good." Cece glanced toward Francie's end of the table. "Maybe we should talk about it more later. I want to keep this between the two of us."

"Totally," I agreed.

"Do you want to walk to my apartment after school? I can explain everything there."

Francie had craned her neck toward us the moment Cece started whispering.

"Sure. My mom will be at work anyway," I said. "Maybe she can drive me home when she leaves Able & Payne."

Francie stood from the table.

"My dad will be home. But he'll be busy with his research project."

Francie walked toward us, stopping to lean down and put both her elbows on the table. She looked from me to Cece and back again.

"Sharing secrets so soon?" Francie asked.

Neither of us responded.

Francie lowered her voice. "Lou has the biggest mouth in sixth grade. I'd be careful if I were you, Cece."

The first time Francie had said my name in twenty-five days.

8

FIRST GRADE

Every Friday night during Lent, the Daughters of Isabella and the Knights of Columbus hosted a parish-wide fish fry in the gym/cafeteria of Our Lady of Perpetual Help. The fish fries were a big deal. Everyone went.

Lent was supposed to be this dark time, at least that's what Father Fred talked about at Mass on Sundays. But you'd never know it if you were at one of those Friday night fish fries. Tommy Maguire's dad blasted music out of the speakers we used for the Christmas play and the spring concert. There was a row of coolers filled with beer and sodas pushed against the wall. The adults talked loudly and laughed even louder. Kids ran around everywhere.

It was at one of those fish fries in first grade where Francie and I invented our secret spying game.

"Want to see if Sister Margaret will give us seconds on brownies?"

We were sitting side by side. Francie's tray held an untouched fried fish fillet and a mound of coleslaw, along with crumbs left over from her first brownie.

Across the room, Mom talked to Nannie and another older woman, who I thought was Annabelle Murphy's grandma. Tripp was strapped to Mom's chest in the baby carrier, with his legs dangling past her waist. He was too big for it, but it was the only way Mom could keep track of him in crowded places. I knew she'd say no to a second brownie.

"I think we're supposed to have one," I said.

"Lou. Sister Margaret won't say no to me."

That was true. Sister Margaret was the school secretary. When Francie got sent to the office, which was often, as long as Sister Margaret was at her desk, Francie got away with a head pat and a hug. Sometimes a lollipop, if Sister Margaret really felt sorry for her.

"I know. But my mom will say no," I said.

"Fine. I'm bored," Francie whined.

The noise and the crowd and the bright overhead lights swirled and made me dizzy. Francie glanced toward the corner of the room where her sister Bernie and a group of third-grade girls played a clapping game.

"We could go play, I guess," Francie said. She stood, but I wanted her to stay. Just the two of us.

"What if we play our own game? We could spy on people." I don't know where the idea came from. Francie leaned in closer, her blue eyes wide, so I continued. "Let's sneak around and listen to people's conversations. They won't even know we're there."

Francie clapped.

"Oh, I love it! Like secret agents."

"Yeah," I said.

First, we staked out the kitchen. The nuns were in charge of the serving line. We hid beside the huge stove. Sister Mary Joseph dropped an entire tray of fish fillets on the floor. She looked around to make sure no one saw, and then, one by one, she put each fillet back on the tray, which she added to the serving line.

Francie snorted. I put a finger to my lips to shush her and we scampered away.

Next, we spotted a group of high school girls gathered around a table by the bathrooms. When we got closer, we could see that the girl in the middle was crying. Fat tears ran down her cheeks. We crawled under the table at the end furthest from them and then inched closer until we could hear what they said.

"He's not worth it. You are so much better than him."

"Totally. Don't give him the satisfaction of seeing you like this."

"Ugh. Boys are the worst."

"Worse than the worst. They're pigs!"

Francie mouthed, "Oink!" She slid out from under the table, and I followed her.

A group of mothers stood near the stage, so we scampered up the steps and behind the curtain. It was hard to hear through the thick fabric, but when I leaned in, I could make it out.

"It's a great turnout, as usual."

"Speaking of turning out, has anyone seen Maureen Fitzpatrick?"

Francie moved closer to the curtain when she heard her mom's name.

"She's not here. It's such a shame how she's always leaving Mike to wrangle those little girls on his own. It's just odd."

I peeked out from the curtain. The voice belonged to Madison Brewer's mom.

"I did see her at Mass recently. She's at the seven a.m. every single morning."

"Even more bizarre!"

I reached into the darkness and found Francie's hand. I pulled her out from behind the curtain, down the stairs, and away from the mothers before we could hear any more.

Francie didn't say anything for a long time. Then, finally, "Let's write this stuff down. So we don't forget."

We grabbed a napkin off a table and found a pen at the abandoned check-in station.

I didn't say anything, I just wrote.

1. Fish fry fish is dirty.

2. Boys are mean.

3. Mrs. Brewer is dumb.

When I finished, I read the list out loud. Francie grinned when I got to number 3. She rolled up the napkin and handed it to me.

"Keep this somewhere safe," she said. "They're our secrets. Just for the two of us. Promise we'll always keep each other's secrets?"

"Promise." Then we shook pinkies.

I was so light, I thought I might float away.

Even after what Francie said about me having a big mouth, even after my heart threatened to explode in my chest, even after I had to count backward twice, I made it through another day at Our Lady of Perpetual Help. The promise of after-school plans with Cece helped.

"What was that about at lunch?" Cece asked as we walked to her apartment. "With Francie."

"I honestly have no clue," I lied.

"Did something happen with you guys? Who would say that out of the blue?"

"Francie," I said quickly. Maybe too quickly. "What I mean is, that's how Francie is. She says things to see how people will react." The lies kept spilling out. "I don't know why she does it, but she's been like that forever."

My face got hot, and I hoped it wasn't turning red. Francie had saved my seat at lunch every day since Sister Mary Joseph's kindergarten class. She'd asked me to be her partner for every school project, so I'd never had to panic about not being picked. She'd slugged Braden behind the slide when he'd made fun of Tripp for wearing a princess cape.

She had also practically started World War III between Madison and Annabelle in fifth grade when she told each of them all the bad things the other had ever said about them. And then there was the day just a week before I said the terrible, horrible things, when she told me I'd never have a boyfriend if I didn't do something about my eyebrows.

So maybe what I said wasn't a lie, but none of it mattered now anyway, and I still felt sick to my stomach.

"Oh, so she's that kind. There was a girl like that at my old school. Always trying to stir stuff up." Cece made a face like she'd bitten into something sour.

I needed to change the subject. "Where was your old school?"

"Columbia. It's only about an hour and a half away. My dad is a professor there. But he grew up here, in Mayfield. He's taking a leave of absence."

We turned onto Market Street and the Missouri River came into view. We passed Market Street Floral and Nettie's Apron. Able & Payne was straight ahead where Market and First Streets intersected.

"My grandmother still lives here. That's why my dad claims we came in the first place. I'm telling you, that makes no sense because he always swore he'd never come back. He hated growing up here." Cece paused and looked over at me. "No offense."

I could relate. "None taken, believe me."

"He's helping my grandmother around her house and working on his research since he's not teaching this semester. But he and my grandmother don't get along *at all*, which is why we never visited. And another reason why moving here makes zero sense! My parents had a big falling-out with her when I was little. I don't know exactly what happened, but my dad only calls her a couple times a year, and my mom refuses to even talk about her." Cece said.

That explained what Opal Duncan had been doing at Able & Payne that day. And why I'd never known she had a granddaughter. In Mayfield, everyone knew everything about everyone. Even the stuff you didn't want to know, as Nannie liked to say.

"So your grandmother is Opal Duncan?" I asked.

"Yep. Do you know her? She's awful."

"Only from seeing her at church. And I saw her with you that day you moved in."

Once we got to Able & Payne, Cece pulled the door open. We stood in the lobby. I could see through the glass door that led into the offices that Mom wasn't at her desk. I followed Cece as she opened another door just to the right. It led to a narrow staircase.

"We have good snacks," Cece said as we climbed. "My dad thinks he'll get me to talk to him by buying me junk food."

Cece used a key to open the door at the top of the staircase.

The sad-eyed man sat at a table drinking coffee and reading a book. He put the book down when we walked in. I could see now that his eyes matched Cece's—round, brown, and kind. I forced myself not to trust the kindness.

"Hi, sweetheart. How was school?" He wore a faded flannel shirt and slippers. He didn't look like a kidnapper. But I guessed I'd never met a kidnapper before.

"It was okay." Cece didn't look at him. Instead, she grabbed two Dr Peppers from the refrigerator and a bag of Cheetos out of a cabinet.

"And you brought a friend. I'm Aaron." He stuck his hand out to me.

"I'm Lou," I said, and grabbed his hand. Cece was already halfway down the hallway. "I go to school with Cece."

"I'm glad you're here, Lou." It sounded like he meant it.

"Well, thanks for having me. And thanks for the snacks." I gestured toward the hallway, where Cece stood holding the Dr Peppers and Cheetos.

"Lou, come on," she said.

I gave Mr. Duncan a wave and then scampered toward Cece.

Cece led us down the hallway and opened a door. Once we were both behind it, she slammed it shut hard enough to make the wall shake a little.

"Easy, Cece!" Mr. Duncan called.

Cece ignored him.

The room wasn't much bigger than a closet. A twin bed with a Missouri Tigers comforter was against one wall, and a white desk and a chest of drawers was against the other. A poster of the signs of the zodiac hung above the desk.

Cece saw me looking at it. "What's your sign?"

"I think I'm a Capricorn? January sixth," I said.

"Yup, Capricorn. I would've guessed that. Explains why you're so serious," Cece said. "My birthday is November twelfth. I'm pretty much a textbook Scorpio."

I didn't know what that meant, but I filed it away in my head to look up later.

"That was your dad? He seems nice." Probably the exact wrong thing to say.

Cece snorted. "I used to think that, too."

She pulled a shoebox out from under her bed. "You'd think if he was going to kidnap me and drag me away from my home, he could've found somewhere nicer. Our house in Columbia was nothing like this. My mom would be horrified if she knew this is where we live."

Cece sat on the floor next to the shoebox. She patted the spot next to her, so I sat down, too. The shoebox was covered with photographs, mostly of Cece. And a woman with dark red hair just a shade darker than Cece's.

"These are the clues I've gathered so far."

Cece held the shoebox tight to her chest. She opened her mouth twice, paused, and then continued. "Before I show you what's in here, there are some things you need to know. First of all, my parents were separating. Not getting divorced. Just separating. That was the plan. But then they had this massive fight, and everything blew up. My mom left for Colorado to stay with my aunt Julie, and the very next day my dad rented a U-Haul and started packing it up."

Cece took a deep breath.

"What did they fight about?" I asked.

Cece chewed on her bottom lip, like she was deciding if she should say more. "I couldn't hear everything. They try not to fight in front of me, but I knew they were talking about me. And at one point my dad yelled, 'Over my dead body!' "

Goose bumps sprung up on my arms.

I waited for her to go on. To explain *what* was over his dead body, but Cece just looked at me expectantly. "And?" I finally asked.

"And." She drew the word out like she was speaking to a small child. "And he meant that over his dead body was I going to live with her instead of him. That's what the fight was about."

Pieces of Cece's story clicked together, and my goose bumps turned to a full-fledged shiver.

"I think he saw an opportunity when she left. He didn't want to risk losing me, so he dragged me here, to the one place she'd never think to look. I've never seen him like that. He usually never gets stressed out, but I'm telling you he was acting so weird."

Cece's eyes were wide. A thousand thoughts were going off like fireworks in my brain, but I couldn't turn them into words, so I just nodded.

"She was only planning to be gone a few days." Cece opened the shoebox lid. "There's stuff in here that proves it."

The first thing she pulled out was a crumpled receipt. Several items were highlighted with a bright pink marker.

"My mom went to the grocery store the day before she left. And not just to make sure we had food while she was gone. She bought things that only she likes." Cece handed me the receipt. "I highlighted them."

Dark Chocolate Almonds
Blonde Roast Coffee
Baked Kale Chips

I set the receipt in my lap. Cece pulled out a folded piece of paper. She unfolded it. It was torn from one of those huge calendars families use to keep track of everyone's schedules. Francie's family had one like it in their kitchen. "September" was across the top in huge type. I had a million questions, but I didn't dare interrupt Cece to ask.

"This is from our calendar. My mom has things scheduled for after her trip. See: she wrote down my dentist appointment. And she wrote that she was supposed to have coffee with someone named Susie on the fourteenth." Cece held the calendar page like she was giving a report, pointing to the boxes as she talked. She handed me the sheet and I set it in my lap with the receipt.

"And look at this email. I found it printed out on my dad's desk in his office." The date was highlighted. "It's the approval for his leave of absence. But the date is right around the time they told me they were separating. He had it all planned out. He was just waiting for his opportunity to get out of town. With me."

She handed me the paper, and I studied it. The story Cece had pieced together certainly made sense. I was glad I'd known better than to trust Mr. Duncan's kind eyes.

Cece kept looking into the shoebox, like she was searching for answers there. When she finally looked up, I got the nerve to break my silence.

"So, what has your dad said? How did he explain this stuff?"

Cece took a deep breath.

"He claims my mom is staying with Aunt Julie for now, and he doesn't know when she'll be back. But the clues I found prove she never planned to be gone long." Cece squeezed the shoebox to her chest so tightly the sides caved in. "When I asked to call her, he said that wasn't a good idea. He said I need to give her time. But he gets shifty whenever I bring her up."

"So, you haven't talked to your mom since she went to Colorado?" I let Cece's words sink in. I tried to wrap my head around weeks passing without speaking to my mom.

"Nope. My dad keeps saying weird stuff, like he's sure she'll reach out to us when she's ready. Meanwhile I know it's a bunch of lies and he brought me here without even telling her. My mom doesn't know where I am. And she has no way to find me."

"Have you tried to call her?"

Cece's eyes were fixed on the floor. "I don't have a cell phone."

That I could understand. I didn't have one either. Mom had an old one that she gave me when I visited Dad in Kansas City. Or spent the night at Francie's house, back when that was a thing I did.

"Plus, I know it's weird," Cece went on, "but I never

memorized her number. If I needed something, I always used my dad's. I stole his phone once to try to find hers, but I couldn't figure out his passcode."

The color in Cece's cheeks turned deeper red. She fidgeted with the edges of her sweater.

"My dad's a Virgo," she said. "Organization is his strength. He knows every detail of my schedule, and he always has his phone. My mom's a Gemini, and Geminis aren't like that. They're too easily distracted."

I didn't know Mom's zodiac sign, but I could relate. James did most of the scheduling at our house, too. He was better at keeping everything straight.

"What about email? Have you tried that?"

"Lou. Really? You don't think I would have already done that if I could?" Cece's cheeks flushed. "I don't know her email address. I used to know her work email, so I tried that. But she lost her job a few months ago, and so the email just bounced back."

My brain turned with ways we could find a working email address or a phone number. But I knew I'd pushed Cece already, and I could brainstorm better once I was home alone with my notebook.

"We'll have to find another way then," I said.

Cece set the shoebox down. "There's one more clue." She reached under her bed and pulled out a thin, light blue pullover sweater. "This is her absolute favorite sweater in the world. She's always cold, so she wears it everywhere. And I mean *every*where. Do you believe someone would leave for good and not even take her favorite sweater?"

Cece held the sweater gently, like it might break if she

wasn't careful. I felt like that with Cece—if I wasn't careful, she might break.

"Cece, do you think maybe—" I chose my words carefully. "Do you think maybe you should tell someone? Like an adult? My mom's not a lawyer but she knows a lot about legal stuff."

"I can't. *We* can't," she said like she'd already considered that option and decided against it.

"Why not? If you think he kidnapped you—"

"Think about what would happen. My dad would get in trouble, right? That wouldn't fix anything. I want my family back. The way it was. If I can find my mom, I know I can fix this. I can fix *us*."

The pit in my stomach grew back into a bowling ball. I thought about my own family. My parents weren't together, but I'd never known another way. Maybe if I had, I'd want that, too.

"Promise me you won't tell anyone, Lou," Cece said. She was still clutching the blue sweater.

I wanted to protect Cece's secrets. I wanted to do what I hadn't done for Francie.

"I promise."

It was as if I were on the bluffs above the river after a storm. Looking down made me dizzy. The water was powerful and dark, and I knew if I went in, it would sweep me away.

10

After Cece tucked her box of clues back under her bed, I promised her I'd do my best. I'd keep her secrets and do whatever I could to help her family. All the while a familiar nagging pulled at my heart. I'd proven myself a terrible secret keeper and an even worse friend.

But maybe if I could figure out how to help Cece, *and* keep her secrets safe, I'd deserve a second chance.

I said a hasty goodbye to Mr. Duncan, who was still hunched over a book at the kitchen table. I avoided his eyes, too afraid of what I might see in them.

Mom was at her desk when I opened the stairwell door into the lobby. I could read the confusion on her face, and she motioned me over.

I pulled the heavy glass door open and stepped into the law offices.

"Cece Clark-Duncan invited me over. We walked here

after school," I answered Mom's question before she had a chance to ask it.

Mom looked thoughtful for a split second, and then she smiled widely. "I'm glad you two are becoming friends. I'll be done here in ten minutes. Want to wait for me in the lobby?"

I nodded and turned back around. I plopped into one of the lobby chairs. The air was hot and heavy, and my legs immediately stuck to the fake, plastic leather. I reached into my backpack for my notebook.

Before I had a chance to get any of the exploding firework thoughts out of my head and onto paper, the front door of Able & Payne swung open. A warm gust of air blew Opal Duncan right in. She smoothed her hair, and before she had a chance to open the door to the stairwell that led upstairs, it creaked open, and Mr. Duncan stepped out.

"Hey Mom," he said, stepping toward her. "Thanks for coming over."

Opal took his hand and squeezed it. "Of course, honey. There's no need for you to weather this storm on your own. How are things today?"

Mr. Duncan pulled his hand away and glanced toward the stairwell door. Then he noticed me sitting there. "Lou, hi. What are you still doing here?"

"My mom works here." I shifted in my seat and motioned toward the glass door. Mom was hunched over her desk. "She's just finishing up."

"I see. Well, I'm glad you could come over today. Come

back anytime." He sought out my eyes, and this time I couldn't avoid it. We made eye contact, and I looked for something that would confirm Cece's story. Something menacing. Or scary. Or shifty. But they were the same as before. Tired, sad, and surprisingly kind.

Opal's eyes were still fixed on her son, as if I wasn't there. She repeated her question. "How are things today?"

Mr. Duncan sighed, made the slightest head nod toward me, and led his mother outside. The kindness in his eyes had almost made me drop my guard, but this move had me back on high alert. He wanted to talk to Opal, and he didn't want me to hear.

I sat sideways in the chair with my notebook open and pretended like I was writing. As discreetly as I could, I snuck glances toward where they stood, deep in conversation. I couldn't hear a thing, but I tried to read their lips, their body language, their hand gestures.

Mr. Duncan threw his hands up like he was exasperated, then turned to walk back inside.

I pulled my knees to my chest and studied my notebook with deep concentration.

Opal followed behind Mr. Duncan, and once again, she didn't notice, or care, that I was there.

"You have to stop beating yourself up, dear. You did what you had to do. What other choice was left?"

I sucked in my breath but kept my eyes trained on my notebook and my hand moving. Anything to keep them from noticing how intently I was listening. I could feel Mr. Duncan's eyes on me.

And then he shushed his mother and hurried her up the stairs.

Despite the heavy, dead air in the law office lobby, I shivered. *You did what you had to do.*

Twenty-nine. Twenty-eight. Twenty-seven.

11

When we got home from Cece's, the first thing Mom did was change her clothes to head out on a run. James was home already, so I wasn't stuck on babysitting duty again.

My nose told me he was there before my eyes did. Garlic and spice hung in the air. The house hugged me in the way it always did when he was cooking something delicious.

"LouLou girl? That you?"

I followed my nose to where James stood manning two pots on the stovetop. He held a wooden spoon in his hand, and he had Orla strapped to his broad chest in her baby carrier. Her head bobbed below his, a miniature version of James. They have the same curly black hair, dark brown skin, and dark eyes that crinkle at the corner when they smile. Tripp looks like them too, but his skin is a few shades lighter, more of a cross between James and Mom.

Orla smiled and babbled like she was James's assistant. Tripp's cartoons blared in the living room.

"Here, give it a taste." James dipped the wooden spoon into one of the pots and held it out to me.

I took a lick off the end. Delicious. Mom's specialty is boxed mac and cheese with sliced hot dogs mixed in. It's a rotating menu of that or something from the freezer when James works the dinner shift at the restaurant, which is most nights. He likes to say Mom's cooking is an embarrassment to real food everywhere. Sometimes, James leaves leftovers from the restaurant in the fridge. And if he works lunch or has the day off, he's in charge of dinner. Those nights are the best.

"Yep, beats the Mom Special," I said.

James laughed. "Still adding in those hot dogs and calling it fancy?"

I laughed, too. It'd been a while since something made me laugh.

"You know some of my secrets. Maybe it's time you take over the dinner shift around here. Your first order of business will be sending those hot dogs straight to the compost."

I laughed again, though it wasn't a bad idea.

"This sauce needs to simmer a minute. Come sit with me. Catch me up on what's been going on. I haven't seen you in days," James said. Orla patted his cheeks with her chubby hands as he talked. He took a seat at the table and pushed out the chair next to him with his foot. I sat.

"How's the restaurant?" I asked before he could ask me any questions.

"Same old, same old. We did add a pasta carbonara to the menu that I think you'll love. First night we don't sell out of it, I'll bring some home for you to try."

I nodded. I wanted to seem excited, but my mind was somewhere else.

"How's Francie?"

I knew that question was coming. Unlike Mom, who was always distracted, James had a pulse on each one of us. I picked at my thumbnail.

"She's fine," I said.

"Huh. Seems like she used to be here nearly as much as you. The last few weekends, I haven't seen or heard anything about her. That girl's hardly the type to go quiet either."

James's eyes were gentle, but questioning.

"I guess we've both been busy." I went back to picking at my nails.

"Okay. If you want to talk about it, you let me know." He smiled, and then kissed the top of Orla's head.

Maybe I should've told James something, but I didn't know what. My mind was a pinball machine pinging back and forth between what I'd done to Francie and what I wasn't sure I could do for Cece.

"You and Francie have been friends for a long time. Friendship is hard, and I can imagine that Francie doesn't make it easier sometimes. But difficult things are worth fighting for. I know you, and I know you'll figure out what to do," James said.

He had it wrong. He thought she was the one who'd done something to me. And I couldn't explain why, but that made me sadder than anything. I didn't have the courage to tell him the real story.

It was silent except for Orla's babbling and Tripp's show blaring in the living room.

James stood and walked back to the stove. I pushed my fight with Francie down, and let Cece's problem bubble to the top.

"There is something I kind of want to talk about. It's not about Francie though."

"You kind of want to talk about it?" James lifted the lid on one of the pots and gave it a good stir.

I spoke before I could stop myself. "There's this new girl. And she has a problem. A pretty big problem. She asked me to help her, and I told her I would. But I don't know if I can. Or if I should."

James looked at me for a few seconds before he said anything. "What kind of problem?"

"I don't think I should say."

James didn't press me. Where Mom would ask me a million questions, he let the silence do the talking. He sat back at the table.

"Well, LouLou girl, it's hard to know what to tell you without more information. So, I'll say this. If someone is in danger, you need to say. Is someone in danger?"

I hesitated. "No. No, nothing like that." I didn't look at James. I thought about Cece's box of clues and how convinced she was that telling someone was not the kind of help she needed. I thought about Mr. Duncan and his kind eyes. But then there were Opal's words. *You did what you had to do.*

Ultimately, I didn't think I was lying. Whatever was happening wasn't good, but Mr. Duncan and Opal wouldn't hurt Cece. And despite being angry, Cece still cared about her dad and what happened to him. I didn't think she was truly in danger.

"Okay, then trust yourself. You're a smart kid and a good friend. And if there's a way you can help this girl, you'll find it."

It was the second time in as many days that someone was wrong about me. I was a lot of things, but good friend was not on the list. I gathered my stuff and started toward my room.

"Thanks, James," I said. "And I'll look into taking over the dinner shift, at least from Mom."

James chuckled. "Deal. Otherwise you're probably stuck with those hot dogs for life."

~

Back in my room, I took my notebook out of my backpack and opened my laptop. Technically, it's Mom's laptop, though she never uses it. It's about a million years old and super slow, but it's better than nothing. Mom got it for college, and then I came along. She'd barely made it a semester before she dropped out and started working behind the counter at Nettie's Apron. She got the job at Able & Payne a few years ago.

A million questions spun around in my head, waiting to get sorted out on paper. I opened the notebook and folded back a fresh page.

The Cece Mystery

1. Is Cece's mom still in Colorado? Find a way to get in touch with someone there.

2. Are Opal and Cece's dad working together? Tell Cece about lobby conversation.

3. Is Cece's dad (or Opal) dangerous? It doesn't seem like it, but need confirmation.

I pushed the notebook to the side and pulled the laptop

in front of me. I entered *parent kidnaps own kid* into the browser.

A list of articles with titles like "What is Parental Kidnapping" and "Consequences of Kidnapping Your Own Child" sprang onto the screen. The articles were full of serious, legal language. My stomach rolled. I was scared, but I'd made a promise.

Thirty. Twenty-nine. Twenty-eight.

I moved the laptop aside and went back to my list.

4. Do whatever it takes to help Cece's family and keep her secrets safe.

I underlined number four three times before I put my notebook away.

12

It had been twenty-six days since I said the terrible, horrible things to Francie, and two days since Cece passed me her note. Thanks to the janky air-conditioning at Our Lady of Perpetual Help and the nerves that swallowed me every time Francie looked in my direction, I was a sweaty mess of sticky polo shirt and frizzy hair.

When I'd arrived at school, Cece was already there. She sat at her desk tapping her foot and writing in her notebook. I knew now that the constellation on the front was the Scorpio constellation. She saw me walk in, dropped her pencil, and met me halfway between the door and the coatroom.

I glanced toward Francie's seat and immediately regretted it. Francie sat on top of her desk surrounded by Madison, Annabelle Murphy, and pretty much every other girl in our class.

"After you left last night, my grandmother came over

for dinner," Cece said. "This whole thing was probably her idea. I can see why my mom hates her, why they *both* hate her."

"Who? Your grandmother?" I was distracted by Francie, who was talking with her hands and laughing loudly.

"Yes, of course my grandmother. Everything makes sense now."

"So you think she's part of it?" I walked into the coatroom. If I couldn't see Francie, maybe I could pretend she wasn't there.

"Yes. All those years we never saw her, she was plotting a way to get between my mom and dad. And she found her perfect opportunity."

I thought of Mr. Duncan and Opal deep in conversation outside Able & Payne. It certainly seemed like they were in this together. And Mr. Duncan might've had problems with his mother at one time, but from what I could tell, he didn't anymore.

Mrs. Jackson interrupted my thoughts before I had a chance to tell Cece what I'd overheard her grandmother say.

"Make your way to your desks. Dr. Morgan's morning announcements start in two minutes."

As soon as we stepped out of the coatroom, I wished we hadn't. Francie was standing at the front of the room.

"Francie, take a seat." Mrs. Jackson motioned toward Francie's desk.

"No problem, Mrs. Jackson. I just have one more invitation to hand out." Francie plunked a pink envelope on Annabelle's desk, then sat at her desk and folded her hands on top.

"Whatever they are, I don't want to hear another word. It's time to start our day," Mrs. Jackson said.

I counted backward as I walked toward my desk. *Three. Two. One.* I willed myself to think about something—anything—other than Francie's twelfth birthday party. What she was thinking about as she made out those invitations. As she planned how she would deliver them.

I slid into my seat, and as I did, I couldn't stop myself from glancing in Francie's direction. We made eye contact, and for that split second, she looked as sad as I felt. Or maybe that's just what I wanted to see. Before I could figure it out, she faced forward and studied the top of her desk like she might find something important in the fake wood grain.

Dr. Morgan's voice droned on, and my body went into autopilot. I stood and folded my hands for the prayer. I put my hand over my heart and recited the Pledge of Allegiance.

"Alright, kiddos. We're going to start our day with some work time for your Christ Is Alive! essays. The goal for today is to select your nominee."

Mrs. Jackson had barely finished giving directions when the room erupted into a chorus of excited whispers and shuffling chairs.

I moved my chair next to Cece's desk. Her Scorpio notebook was out and open, but when I got there she shoved it in her desk.

"Now remember this is a member of the community who deserves recognition for their contributions. Use this time to share your ideas. Try to come up with someone you *both* admire," Mrs. Jackson said over the noise.

Part of our homework the night before had been to brainstorm a list of people we were interested in interviewing. I took mine out and set it on Cece's desk.

"We could do Ms. Nettie. She owns the bakery. It's close to your apartment. Have you been there yet?" Ms. Nettie was my top choice, and I figured Cece would agree. "She donates any leftover baked goods to the food pantry each day. And they have the absolute best donuts. I'm sure she'd let us have some for free while we interview her."

"I don't know," Cece said. "She seems like kind of an obvious choice. I bet at least three other groups are thinking about those free donuts."

She had a point. I didn't want to turn in the same project as Tommy and Braden.

"What about Mr. Able? His office is right under you, and my mom could help us set up an interview." Mr. Able scared me, but Mom told me that he took on cases for free, which probably qualified as a "Christlike contribution to the community."

"What about Angel Sweeney?" Cece asked.

"Angel Sweeney? You mean the psychic?"

Angel Sweeney lived in a house with a big wraparound porch across the street from Mayfield Municipal Park. A wooden sign in her yard advertised her business.

"Yes. Her. But she's an astrologer and tarot card reader."

"Same difference."

"Not really. Psychics claim they have a special gift that connects them to the other side. Astrologers use scientific information, like the solar system and the positions of planets. That's why they can get way more specific with dates and information. They're not the same."

"I still don't think it qualifies as 'Christlike.'"

There was no way Mrs. Jackson would approve this idea.

"Of course it does. She helps people. Isn't that the whole point of this thing?" Cece said.

I'd seen Angel around town a few times, but I didn't know much about her. On Halloween in third grade, Francie had dared me to ring Angel's doorbell. It had shocked Francie when I'd run right up and done it. Angel had answered the door in a bathrobe and handed me a Hershey's bar.

"Now you go," I had said when I got back to Francie waiting on the sidewalk.

"No way!" Francie said. "That lady gives me the creeps. And my mom said she channels spirits and stuff." Francie shuddered.

"You believe that?" Angel seemed as safe as anyone else handing out candy that night.

"I don't know, but I do think she's scary." Nothing scared Francie, so it had been my turn to be shocked.

"I'm hearing lots of great ideas," Mrs. Jackson cut through my thoughts. "Is there a group that would like to share their choice?"

Francie's hand shot up.

"Francie, who have you and Madison selected?"

"We're going to interview Madison's mom. She's the cheerleading coach at Riverside Community College and she also coaches Madison's traveling cheer team."

I wanted to gag. If anyone was going to be considered "Christlike" for this project, it should *not* have been

Madison's mom. Mrs. Brewer was the grown-up version of Madison—perfectly styled hair, too-tight jeans, and a habit of asking questions that sounded concerned but were actually insulting.

"Excellent. Anyone else?" Mrs. Jackson said.

Francie and Madison smiled at each other. I remembered how Francie had looked at me when I'd been braver than her that Halloween. I raised my hand.

"Louise, share, please."

"We're going to do Angel Sweeney." I regretted it immediately, but I knew I couldn't stop there. "She's an astrologer. And also a tarot card reader. Which is interesting. And also helpful. To the community." Heat rose in my face, and I wanted to hide under the desk. I glanced over at Cece, and she smiled.

"I think we're going to learn a lot from our choice," Cece said. She pulled her ponytail tighter and sat up straight.

"That is an interesting choice, but I'm going to need to think about it. See me at lunch, please," Mrs. Jackson said.

I expected Francie to whisper to Madison or stare out the window while I talked. But she studied Cece instead.

~

After the loud chatter of our essay partner work, Mrs. Jackson instructed us to return to our seats and take out our vocabulary workbooks.

"Sixth graders, let's quiet our minds and get them ready for the rest of the day. Open your workbooks to page thirty-five."

I was on number five when Mrs. Fleming walked in.

"Francie, are you ready?" she asked.

My body tensed. Madison and Annabelle exchanged a

knowing look. Francie's face turned pink. The whole class stared at her as she pulled a folder out of her desk.

She clenched her jaw. "Don't be jealous because I get to miss class."

Madison and Annabelle exchanged another look.

I put my head down and focused on my workbook, praying for about the millionth time in twenty-six days that I could rewind time. That I could make Francie's secrets safe again. That I could give her a thumbs-up under the table, and she'd wink as she waved to the class and walked out the door. Instead, she straightened her shoulders and followed Mrs. Fleming without turning around.

13

SECOND GRADE

I slept over at Francie's for the first time when we were in second grade.

Mom dropped me off right before dinner. I had a sleeping bag we'd bought at Goodwill slung over one shoulder and my backpack slung over the other. Francie sat on the porch steps waiting for me.

She popped up as soon as I closed the car door.

"Come on." She took the sleeping bag out of my arm and led me inside before I could feel even a teensy bit sad about leaving Mom for the night.

Francie's house smelled like church and had more pictures of saints and crosses on the walls than the halls at Our Lady of Perpetual Help. There was a whole bookshelf filled with pictures and statues of the Virgin Mary. I figured that's where Mrs. Fitzpatrick had prayed for the girl babies. Francie and her sisters were wilder than any pack of boys, though, so I wasn't sure all that praying had worked out the way she'd wanted it to.

We went back to the bedroom Francie shared with Bernie, and Francie threw my sleeping bag on her bed.

"What do you want to do?" Francie asked.

We both knew the answer, so before I could respond, Francie said, "Secret Spies?"

One of the great things about Francie's house was that the possibilities for spying were endless. She didn't have to ask anyone's permission to do anything. Her dad was always at work, and even when her mom was home and not at church, I barely ever saw her. Whatever she was doing, Francie never wanted to bother her.

I'd just finished reading Harriet the Spy, so I had brought an official notebook to use for the game. I'd just pulled it out of my overnight bag, when the screen door creaked open.

"Hey, Mom, Mackenzie's here! We're walking downtown for ice cream," Bernie yelled from the living room.

No one answered, and the screen door slammed shut.

Francie's eyes twinkled. She leaned forward with her elbows on her knees. "Bernie's going to be gone for a while. Let's go through her drawers and see if we can find anything juicy."

"We should start with her underwear drawer. My mom keeps old letters in hers," I said.

Francie giggled. "See, everyone at school thinks you're the nice one. But deep down you're as bad as me." Francie opened the top drawer of Bernie's dresser and pulled out a training bra. She held it to her chest. "Ooh la la, Bernie's getting ta-tas," she sang.

I fell to the floor laughing. Then I opened our notebook and wrote:

Bernie's Underwear Drawer

1. Training bra—she's getting ta-tas.

I was just like Harriet.

Francie dug back into the drawer and when she came up, she held Bernie's diary. It had a lock, but one of those locks that's only on there to make kids think their private thoughts are actually private. We popped it right open.

"You read it. Out loud," Francie commanded.

I cleared my throat and tried my best to sound like Bernie. "Dear Diary, I think Mason Brewer is cute, but Mackenzie likes him, too."

Francie made a face. "Oh my God. That's disgusting. Keep reading."

"You read." I shoved the diary toward Francie. "If she gets home soon, I don't want to be the one holding it."

Francie shoved it back to me. "No, you read. You were doing a good job."

"Who cares? You read it. I'm scared," I said.

"I don't want to read it. You do it."

"If no one wants to read, let's put it away."

Francie pulled the book back from me. "Fine. I'll do it." She stared at the page. But she stumbled over the first two words. Before she got to the third, she threw the diary at me. "Are you happy now? Not everyone is a brainiac like you, Lou." Her voice quivered. "Besides, Bernie's handwriting is horrible, and the words keep jumping off the page."

I didn't know what to say, so I grabbed the diary. I opened it and read the next entry.

~

I learned about Francie's secret classes a few days after the sleepover. We sat under the rusty slide.

"Since you found out my secret, I'm going to tell you everything," Francie said. "But you have to swear you'll never tell anyone."

I nodded. If Francie told me a secret, I'd lock it up tight and throw away the key.

"No, Lou. This is serious. It's not like the notebook secrets. I need to hear you say it."

"Okay. I swear."

"Swear on the Holy Bible, and everything you own, and your granddad's grave."

I paused a second too long.

"Lou, say it or I won't tell you."

I swore. I even held my right hand with three fingers raised like a Girl Scout.

"I have a learning problem. Sister Mary Alice figured it out. She had me take this test. That's why I have to leave class sometimes."

"Where do you go?" Francie had told everyone she didn't need to learn the stuff we were learning so they let her be an office helper.

"With Mrs. Fleming. We do reading practice. But it's not helping. The letters and words get jumbled in my head. Sometimes they look like they're flying off the page."

"I'm sure Mrs. Fleming will help you figure it out."

"She says people learn in different ways, and she's trying to get me what I need. But I know what that means. I'm dumb."

I wanted to tell her that wasn't true. She was the smartest kid I knew. But somehow the words got stuck, and I asked her a pointless question instead.

"What did your mom say?"

"She just said okay and didn't bring it up again. But I'm sure she's embarrassed. Bernie is a total pain but at least she's smart. Straight A's and all that."

"I'm sure your mom's not embarrassed of you," I said.

"Please, please, Lou. Don't tell anyone. I would die if anyone found out."

I nodded, promising her secret was safe with me. Then we shook pinkies. "I pinky swear, and I swear on the Holy Bible, and I swear on everything I own, and, and . . . I swear on my granddad's grave."

That afternoon, Mrs. Fleming's gravelly voice came over the intercom. "Send Francie Fitzpatrick down, please."

As Francie stood, she glanced over at me. I gave her a thumbs-up under my desk. She did an exaggerated curtsy and said, "Don't be jealous! I'll be back soon."

She stood in the doorway, blew a kiss to the class, and danced her way into the hallway.

Cece and I spent lunchtime convincing Mrs. Jackson that Angel Sweeney was a worthy choice for our essay.

"Astrology is not like talking to spirits or anything, Mrs. Jackson," Cece began. "It's science. Astrologers use the stars and planets to help people understand their lives better."

"We use God for that, Cece," Mrs. Jackson said.

"Okay. But tons of Catholic people from history have relied on astrology, like popes and saints, and even the Three Wise Men. How else do you think they knew how to use that star to find Jesus?"

Mrs. Jackson was still skeptical, but I was impressed.

"And Angel helps people. Maybe you don't believe in it, but there are people out there who do, and that should count for something, right?"

"I'm not sure Dr. Morgan or Father Fred will see it that

way." Mrs. Jackson hesitated just enough to make me think we had a window.

"It's a contest, though, right? So maybe you and the judges won't decide that Angel is the *most* Christlike, but that doesn't mean we can't learn something," I spoke up.

Mrs. Jackson studied us.

"And we'll include the Catholic history stuff Cece is talking about in our essay, to make sure Jesus really gets in there, you know?"

Mrs. Jackson sighed.

"Okay, fine. I will expect to see a clear connection between Catholicism and astrology. Got it?"

We both nodded and left the classroom before she had time to change her mind. We were lucky Mrs. Jackson wasn't a nun. A nun definitely would've said no.

~

Once Mrs. Jackson gave us the go-ahead to do our project on Angel, we decided to start that afternoon. Cece said her dad had gone to Cairo for the afternoon—something related to his research, but she wasn't sure what—so he'd arranged for her to go to Opal's after school.

"If that's not suspicious, I don't know what is. He doesn't trust me to be alone for a few hours? I'm almost twelve years old."

I agreed. Mom left me home alone all the time, and with an ornery five-year-old and sassy one-year-old half the time, too.

Opal picked us up in a dusty green pickup truck. It didn't match the Opal I knew from Sunday Mass. That Opal wore her gray hair in a tight bun, not a hair out of place, and her long skirts were creased just so, freshly ironed that morning. When she pulled into Our Lady of Perpetual Help, her hair was still tight, but she wore jeans and a loose button-down shirt.

Cece hopped in next to her grandmother without saying a word, and I squeezed in beside her.

"How was your day, Cecelia? Are you going to introduce me to your friend? She's about to be a guest in my home, after all."

"This is Lou." Cece kept her body turned toward me and the passenger side window.

"Hi." I leaned forward and gave Opal a wave.

"Cecelia, your manners are unseemly. But I guess that's what years of limited parenting does to a child. If you would like to bring home a guest, please introduce her properly."

Cece rolled her eyes and mouthed, "See what I mean?" Then she turned toward her grandmother and spoke slowly and deliberately like she was talking to a small child. "Grandma. This is my friend. Her name is Lou Bennett. She goes to my school."

I reached my hand out to shake Mrs. Duncan's. "It's nice to meet you." Though I wasn't sure it was.

We rode the rest of the way in silence. Opal Duncan lived by herself where the paved roads turn to gravel, in an old white house with a goat and some chickens. My mom said she only came to town for groceries and Sunday Mass. I saw her every Sunday, but this was the first time I'd ever spoken to her.

Opal's house was full of sharp edges and hard surfaces,

and it smelled like the library. The living room was sparse and clean, which made the pictures pop out at me. Shelves and walls were full of photographs of what had to be Cece's dad— a chubby baby splashing in an old-fashioned bathtub, a round-faced toddler on a tricycle, a kid about my age holding up a trophy, a teenager in a cap and gown. Sprinkled between the boy-versions of Mr. Duncan were pictures of Cece, too—at a beach, in the mountains, eating a Popsicle. It was like a shrine to a family Cece said Opal never really knew.

I scanned the room looking for a picture of Cece's mom, but I only found her in one. She was in the background of a photo focused on a smiling Mr. Duncan carrying a toddler Cece on his shoulders.

"I'll be in my garden," Opal said. "Feel free to work at the kitchen table or in the study. There's a computer if you need it. But if you want to go outside, come to the back where I'll be able to see you."

Cece rolled her eyes. She didn't respond to her grandmother. Instead, she grabbed my arm and pulled me toward the study.

"I told you. Awful," Cece said as soon as we heard the back door open and shut. "She's always like that."

"She's a little harsh," I agreed. "And it's definitely weird how she wants to watch over you like that."

Most kids I knew had the run of the town, and no one worried about us as long as we made it home in time for dinner.

"It's like they want to make sure I don't run away," Cece said, and I shivered.

Cece sat down in the desk chair in front of a massive,

ancient-looking desktop computer. I sat across the room in a stiff armchair and pulled out my leather-bound notebook and my school notebook, ready to change the subject to our project.

"So how did you find out about Angel?" I asked.

"I was walking around, kind of exploring Mayfield one day, and I saw her place. I got into astrology a few years ago. I was honestly pretty surprised to see Mayfield has an astrologer."

"You know a lot about it, huh."

"I guess so. I think it's cool, and I think you'll like it, too. There's something reassuring about it. Like despite how out of control things might seem, there's an order to everything. The universe actually does make sense."

I wanted order in my universe. And for my life to make sense. But I wasn't convinced astrology was the answer.

"I think Angel might be able to help us, too," Cece continued.

"What do you mean?"

"It's part of the reason I wanted to pick her in the first place. She'll be able to give me some answers."

"About your mom?"

"Yeah."

Cece stared straight ahead. I didn't think Angel Sweeney had Cece's answers, but I couldn't say that out loud. Instead, I said a silent prayer that she'd find them. Somewhere.

~

We googled Angel Sweeney and got a link to her website, articles that had been written about her in newspapers in Mayfield and Columbia, and her Facebook page. Angel seemed well-known in her world, which I knew nothing about. Cece was impressed by her credentials, too.

"Oh wow. She writes the horoscopes for the papers around here. We should read ours. If she's as good as her website says she is, we might be able to learn something important from them."

I'd never checked my horoscope in a newspaper. One of the last times I spent the night at Francie's, though, she'd gathered a bunch of Bernie's magazines—old copies of *People* and *Us Weekly*. After looking for updates on her celebrity crushes, Francie had turned to the back to find the horoscopes.

"Maybe it will tell me if I'm going to have a boyfriend in sixth grade," Francie had said.

"You know that stuff is made up, right?" I'd said.

"Okay, fine." Francie had closed the magazines and set them on Bernie's bed. We'd gone downstairs to watch a movie. I had tried my best to focus on the screen and not all the ways Francie was changing.

"Lou, look at this." Cece's voice brought me back to Opal's study and Angel Sweeney. "We have to get her to give us a reading." She was on a page titled "Astrology Readings." She used the cursor to highlight a few lines.

Life is uncertain. Do you ever wish it came with a road map? Something to tell you why things have happened in your life and what you can expect to happen next? Welcome to the power of astrology!

"This is exactly what I need," Cece whispered.

I fiddled with my leather-bound notebook— it begged to be opened. If we were going to do this, we needed a real plan. I took a deep breath and dove in. "Where do you think your mom might be?"

"I don't know." Cece spoke slowly. "At our house in Columbia, looking for clues about where we went. Or maybe when she got home, and found us gone, she went back to my aunt Julie's. Either way, I know she must be worried."

"I'm sure she is." I imagined Mom spending weeks not knowing where I was. "Do you think she'll eventually look here? Since your grandmother lives here? Even though they weren't on great terms, it seems like your grandma was keeping up with you," I said, thinking of the living room full of photographs.

"I told you, Lou. They *hate* each other. And my dad felt the same way. He talked all the time about how glad he was to have gotten out of Mayfield. This is the *last* place she would think he'd bring me."

I could understand why someone would leave Mayfield and never come back. But whatever his reason, Mr. Duncan eventually *had*.

Cece pulled the sleeves of her uniform sweater over her hands. She chewed on her bottom lip and kept her eyes focused on the computer screen.

I got a little braver with each question, so I pressed on. "What about the police? Are you sure you aren't in over your head with this?"

"It's like I told you yesterday. I'm mad at my dad, but I don't want something bad to happen to him. That wouldn't fix anything. The only way to undo this is to find my mom myself."

Sometimes it's too late to undo what's been done. I would know. But, maybe it could be different for her. Maybe I could help make things different for her.

Cece paused and took a deep breath. "If she doesn't find me soon, though, that might be the only option."

"Yeah, maybe."

I imagined us traipsing into the Mayfield Police Department. Would they arrest Mr. Duncan right away? What if they couldn't find Cece's mom? My breath caught in my throat.

"Then you're right. We have to find her ourselves." I tried to sound more sure of myself than I felt. I wanted more than anything to help Cece, help her family, but it was hard to shake the uncertainty that pulled at my heart.

"There's one more clue I didn't tell you about the other day. She had a trip planned for us. A trip to San Francisco. Geminis love to travel—she's a Gemini, you know—and San Francisco is her absolute favorite, so she was planning to take me there with her. *This* fall. She got travel books and showed me all her favorite places and everything. Someone with a trip like that planned wouldn't up and take off. Would they?"

Cece turned, and she looked me in the eye for the first time since we'd started talking about her mom. She looked breakable. If I said the wrong thing, she might crumble right in front of me.

"No, of course they wouldn't."

~

We found Angel's email address on her website. We worked together to craft a message that explained our project and requested a meeting, but we left out the exact title of the project. That was Cece's idea. Too much Jesus-talk might turn her off right away.

As I clicked send, I thought of something.

"This is a total invasion of privacy, so tell me no if you don't want to." I couldn't believe it'd taken me so long to think of something so obvious. "But what if we do a little digging on this computer?"

Cece didn't hesitate. "You're brilliant, Lou, and that's a brilliant plan."

It was easier than I could've hoped for. There were no open tabs, but when we went to gmail.com, Opal's username and password were saved, and we got right in. We had to filter through dozens of spam emails and ads—it was like she'd signed up for emails from every website she'd ever visited—and then, on the second page of her inbox, we found it.

An email from aaron.duncan@mail.missouri.edu. Subject line: Just in case

"Open it! Open it!" Cece shriek-whispered.

I held my breath and clicked it open.

Found this in my files. No expiration, and we might need it depending on how long we need to stay.

The words pulled the air right out of my lungs. There was an attachment, and before I could think, I opened that, too.

Power of Attorney for Cecelia Clark-Duncan, minor child

I didn't understand what I was looking at, and before I could read on, the back door creaked open.

"Oh my god. Close it," Cece whispered.

I closed Opal's email account, but before I closed the attachment, I hit the printer icon. Opal's dusty printer sputtered to life.

"Lou! What are you doing?" Cece's eyes were saucers.

We could hear Opal clattering around in the room next to the study.

The paper shot out, and I shoved it in my backpack just as Opal's head popped through the doorway.

"Are you two about done in here? I can give you a ride home whenever you're ready."

Cece reached for my hand and squeezed it. "We got a lot done. I'm so lucky to be working on this with Lou."

I was dizzy and the river whirred through my ears, but I squeezed back.

15

The Cece Mystery: Things I Know For Sure
1. Cece hasn't seen or talked to her mom in three weeks.
2. Cece's dad and grandma are acting _very_ suspiciously.
3. Cece has lots of proof that her mom was planning to come back from her aunt's house (shoebox clues, trip to California)
4. Cece believes that Angel Sweeney can help her.
5. Cece believes that I can help her.

I stared at this list in my notebook on Thursday morning, while I was supposed to be writing in my Language Arts journal. I had my journal open on top of my desk and my notebook open inside it. When Mrs. Jackson looked in my direction, I grabbed my pencil and acted like I was furiously writing.

Mrs. Jackson called our journals Seed Journals. We were supposed to use them to write about little "seed stories" instead of big "watermelon topics." She promised the little seed moments put together would show us who we are. I didn't buy it. Plus, practically every special little moment I could think of included Francie, so journal writing was one of my least favorite parts of the day.

Cece didn't feel the same way. I'd noticed that every time Mrs. Jackson announced it was time to pull out our Seed Journals, Cece scrambled to get hers out. She wrote and didn't stop until time was up. Sometimes she went past that.

Today was no exception. She probably wrote about her mom. And that made me feel like counting backward.

Francie sat ahead of me, near the windows. She held her head in one hand, and by the way the other hand moved, I knew she was doodling instead of writing.

Last night when I'd gotten home from Opal's, I'd locked myself in my room with the attachment from Mr. Duncan's email. It was a legal document, a lot like the documents that spilled out of Mom's work bag, and the professional language was hard to understand. The date at the top was from nine years ago, and from what I could figure out, it gave Opal Duncan permission to make decisions for Cece—about school, doctors, travel. The stuff parents were responsible for. It was signed by Aaron Duncan.

I hadn't dared show it to Mom, but I knew she would know what it meant, so I had asked her about it while she was doing the dinner dishes.

"Mom, do you know what a power of attorney is?"

"Of course. Do you? Where is this coming from?"

"Nowhere." I felt my face turning pink. "Just a show I was watching. What is it? Like if a grandparent has one for a kid?"

"Were you watching *Law & Order* reruns with Francie again? I know she doesn't have a lot of TV rules, but you do. That stuff will give you nightmares."

I was relieved Mom was on the wrong track. She'd answer my questions without asking too many of her own.

"This episode wasn't scary. No murders or anything. Just custody stuff," I said.

"I thought they all had a murder." Mom poured detergent into the dishwasher.

"Not this one," I said quickly. "So what is it?"

"It gives someone power to make decisions for someone else. Typically you would only have one for a child if the parents will be away for a long time or are unable to be reached for some reason. Where were the parents on the show?"

"Colorado," I answered before I could think. And before Mom had a chance to respond, I had turned on my heels and gone back to my room, shutting the door behind me.

Mrs. Jackson's journal-writing music droned on and brought me back to the classroom. I started a second list in my notebook.

The Cece Mystery: Questions

1. How can we find Cece's mom's phone number? Hack her dad's phone? (learn how to hack a phone?) Does he have it written down somewhere?

2. What is the power of attorney for and why did they have one nine years ago? How does it fit with what's happening now?

3. Aunt Julie—what does she know and how can we get in touch with her?

I couldn't make the pieces fit together in a way that made sense. It was like one of Tripp's puzzles when Mom made him clean his room on his own—a bunch of random pieces shoved into boxes that stood no chance of making a finished product.

Mrs. Jackson slowly turned the music down. She didn't want to use a timer because it might disrupt our creativity.

"Okay writers, finish your thought. I'll know you're ready to move on when your journals are back inside your desks. Take your time. Don't leave important thoughts hanging."

I shut my journal and slammed it back into my desk. Cece wrote for at least another two minutes without looking up. Mrs. Jackson was true to her word, though. She didn't move on until Cece closed her journal and placed it back in her desk.

"Glad that's over," Francie said. She was talking to Madison, but she said it loudly enough that the whole class heard.

Braden leaned across the aisle toward Francie and her journal. "What were you working on, Francie? Tracing the ABCs?"

Madison turned and stared, wide-eyed. Tommy dug through his desk, like he didn't hear. I tried not to throw up.

Cece stood. She fanned her nose wildly. Her seat was directly behind Braden's.

"Ugh, Francie, clearly Braden did not take your advice about deodorant. Mrs. Jackson, can I move? Something stinks back here."

Francie scooted her desk away from Braden and closer to Madison.

"Yeah, Mrs. Jackson. We might need to have the custodians take a look around. It smells like something died." Francie pinched her nose.

"Girls, that's enough. And, Mr. Kelly, I'll see you inside during lunch," Mrs. Jackson broke in.

A weird mixture of intense gratitude and jealousy swirled around inside me. I was glad someone had rescued Francie, but I wasn't sure I was glad Cece was the one to do it.

"Let's switch gears to our Christ Is Alive! projects," Mrs. Jackson said, and the class started moving.

When I was situated next to Cece, I couldn't help myself.

"What was that all about?" I asked.

"What was what all about?"

"It's not a great idea to get on Braden's bad side." I felt a pang of guilt for wishing Cece had stayed quiet.

"Someone had to say something. The way Braden keeps making those cracks about Francie, and really *everyone*, is disgusting. He shouldn't get away with that."

The room spun. I worried Cece could hear the pounding in my chest. *Thirty. Twenty-nine. Twenty-eight.* I knew she was right. And I wanted Braden to stop more than anyone. But I also had that feeling about Cece that I'd had about Francie—if I didn't hold on tight, she'd slip away.

"One of my best friends at my old school has ADHD. This jerk in our class always made rude comments when she had to go to the nurse's office to take her medicine. I guess Braden reminds me of him. And no one deserves that," Cece continued.

"You're right. Braden is the worst," I managed to say, before changing the subject. "Did you ever hear back from Angel?"

"I haven't had a chance to check. Maybe we can go to the library after school. That is if my dad and grandma are willing to let me out of their sight," Cece said.

"And maybe we can work on figuring out your mom's email? Or try to get in touch with someone else who might have her number?"

"Yes, for sure. I've been trying to think of a list of other people who might be able to help us."

"Let's talk about this later. At the library," I said.

I had the feeling Francie was watching us. I didn't think she could hear us from where she sat, but I didn't want to take any chances.

"Okay. Back to Angel," Cece said. She pushed her sleeves past her elbows.

She moved the interview question list in front of her. As she wrote, a note folded into the shape of a heart slid across the room. It landed next to Cece's black Converse sneaker.

Cece—written across the front in handwriting as familiar as my own.

Cece grabbed the note and looked toward where it came from. Francie's back was to us. She was deep in conversation with Madison.

Cece carefully unfolded the note and I read it over her shoulder.

That was really cool of you. Braden stinks. Thank you. —FF

16

Cece got permission from her dad, and we went to the library on Thursday afternoon. Cece had an email from Angel waiting in her school inbox.

Cecelia—

I am available on Tuesday afternoon. I can meet with you briefly. I hope you are as serious about astrology as you say you are.

Be well,

Angel

The next Tuesday, we met in front of the buses after school and walked the six blocks to Angel's house.

"We need to make a good impression," Cece said as we walked. "I'm counting on getting a free reading out of this."

"Have you had a reading before?" I was a little freaked out by the idea.

"Once. My mom let me go to an astrologer in Kansas

City. I know you think it's strange, but once you see for yourself, you'll be hooked."

"I just feel like it's telling people what they want to hear and charging money for it. I'll have to see it to believe it, I guess."

"Maybe you will. With Angel, if she's anything like the astrologer in Kansas City. She was incredible. Have you ever been to Kansas City?"

"My dad lives there." I don't know why I hadn't told Cece this yet. It's not like it's a secret. But if I don't talk about it, I don't have to think about it. And sometimes, *most* of the time if I'm being honest, I'd rather not think about it.

I felt Cece studying my face. "Your parents are divorced?"

"Never married. They were young." Heat crept up my neck. I hated myself for feeling embarrassed.

"What's it like?" Cece asked. She stopped walking. "Having parents that don't live together? Who don't even live in the same place?"

I stopped and looked Cece in the eye. Maybe I should've lied— "It's no big deal"—or glossed over the question— "It's fine"—but instead, I told the truth.

"It's hard sometimes. Like when my dad has to miss things other dads are there for, or when it feels like we're not as close as maybe we would've been."

Cece nodded. I could tell she was considering every word I said.

"But there are good things, too. Like my mom is married now. And my stepdad is great. And my brother and sister—I wouldn't have them if things were different."

Cece nodded again, but she didn't say anything.

We walked in silence for the next block.

"Thanks for telling me all that," Cece said finally.

This time I nodded and didn't say anything. We kept walking.

"I talked to my mom about that document we found on your grandma's computer," I said.

Cece stopped. "You showed it to her?" There was panic in her eyes.

"Oh no, of course not. I told her I heard about power of attorney on TV."

Cece started walking again. "Okay. Good. And? What did she say?"

"She said it's something you need if you're separated from your parents. Did you ever stay with your grandma for a long time when you were little?"

"I don't remember that, and I have a very good memory." She chewed on her bottom lip. "But I've been thinking about it, and maybe it's because my dad and my grandma tried this before. Maybe this isn't the first time they came up with this plan. It's just the first time it worked."

The hair on my arms stood on end. As terrible as it sounded, it made sense. Maybe Mr. Duncan and Opal had been plotting something like this for years. "You're sure you don't remember anything?"

"Not a thing." Cece tightened her ponytail, and we found ourselves outside Angel's house.

The paint was chipped on the wooden sign in her yard, and the wraparound porch sagged in a few places. Cece rang the bell.

A dog barked. We could hear feet padding down the hall and the clip of dog nails on hardwood.

The door swung open. Angel stood in front of us. Her black hair was swept into a tight bun on the top of her head. Her eyebrows were two thick black lines that made her expression hard to read. She wore a brightly printed robe over jeans and a white T-shirt. She pulled it around herself and held the dog's collar.

"This is Mercury," she said, patting the hound dog. He sat at her feet panting. "Can I assume you are Cecelia and Louise?"

"Yes. Cece and Lou." Cece stuck her hand out for Angel to shake.

Angel reached her hand from where she knelt next to Mercury and grabbed Cece's. Then she stood and walked back into her house.

"Nicknames. How sweet. Come in."

We followed her into the front room. It smelled like the incense Father Fred flung around the church during the Holy Week masses. The furniture looked like it came from River City Antiques downtown. Angel settled onto the couch and Mercury lumbered next to her. She gestured for Cece and me to take the two armchairs sitting opposite. I perched on the edge of one, and Cece took the list of questions out of her bag and sat in the other chair.

"How'd you come up with the name Mercury?" I figured that was a good place to start. People with dogs usually love talking about their dogs.

"Lou." Cece gave me a look. I could tell she thought it was a dumb question.

"Pluto was taken," Angel said. Her tone was sarcastic, but she winked at me, so I didn't feel stupid.

"Mercury is an astrology name," Cece said. "Mercury is the messenger of the gods. In astrology, it's why we think the way we do."

"Ah. Impressive. I see you do know a few things," Angel said.

She raised her stick-straight eyebrows and smiled at Cece.

"Tell me more about why you're here."

I nodded at Cece to take the lead. Angel was ready to listen to her.

"We have this project at school. To interview someone who's made a positive impact on the community." Cece still left out the Jesus stuff. Smart.

"There's a presentation at the end of the quarter, and one of the essays gets named the winner. Parents come and watch, and all that. But you would only come if we won. And I'm not sure we have much of a chance of winning."

"Why do you think you won't win? I'm extremely interesting." Angel winked again. Neither of us said anything. "Is it correct that this is a project for the Catholic school?"

Cece and I exchanged a look. We both nodded. Slowly.

"And your teacher has approved your essay idea?"

We nodded again.

"Us Catholics are into lighting candles and rituals and believing in stuff you can't see, so if you ask me, they'll love astrology. They just might not know it yet," I offered.

Angel's smile disappeared.

"I'm not worried about them. I'm worried about you. What I do is not a joke or a spectacle. Do you understand?"

I nodded. I was afraid to open my mouth again.

"Of course it's not a joke. I already know a lot. I've read lots of books and I've had my birth chart read and everything." Cece shot me a look.

"So what about you?" Angel pointed one of her black polished fingernails at me. "You seem less sure."

I tensed. She was right.

"She's sure. She's just a total Capricorn. Even her moon sign is Capricorn. You know how that goes—super serious."

I had no idea what Cece was talking about, but I nodded along like I did.

"I see," Angel said.

We sat in silence for at least a solid minute. I wanted to walk right out the door. We could still interview Mr. Able.

Not Cece, though. She scooted to the edge of her seat.

"I'm sure this doesn't seem important to you. But it's important to us. *Really* important." Cece's voice was desperate.

"We could help with your business," I said. "And advertising. We want to learn from you, and we'd be willing to do more than the interview."

Angel still looked skeptical.

"And our teacher approved the project. She agreed that what you do is valuable to the community. You can email her." Part of that was true, at least.

"Please. Whatever you want help with, we'll do it. *Please*." Cece leaned so far forward, she almost fell out of her chair.

Maybe Angel wanted our help. Maybe she would email Mrs. Jackson. Or, maybe Angel sensed there was more to Cece's request than the school project. And maybe Angel wanted to fix the desperation in Cece's voice as badly as I did.

"What do you think, Mercury? Should we do it?" Angel scratched Mercury behind the ears. Mercury groaned. "That settles that, then. Mercury is a good judge of character. I'll do it. But I have a newspaper deadline this afternoon, so we'll have to save the interview for another day."

"That's fine. We have plenty of time," I said. "Thank you so much. We promise we'll do a good job."

"Yes, thank you." Cece pressed her hands together. Her grin broke her face wide open.

Angel stood. Mercury plodded off the couch after her.

"And I may take you up on your offer to help out around here. I could use the extra hands."

We followed Angel to the door.

"In the meantime, Cece, please work on Lou here." Angel winked at me once more, and a smile snuck across her face. "I sense skepticism in her aura."

17

By Thursday, we were at a standstill. We hadn't heard back from Angel about rescheduling the interview. I worried that we wouldn't have the interview done in time. I knew how badly Cece wanted this, so when she urged me to be patient, I tried my best.

We also hadn't made much headway on Cece's mystery. I kept thinking there was something we were missing. Cece had tried a few things, but maybe she hadn't tried hard enough. There had to be a way to make contact with her mom. Especially if she was out there somewhere trying to do the same thing.

After school on Thursday, I was alone in my bedroom. Mom was at work and Tripp and Orla were still at daycare. I lay on my bed and wrote in my notebook.

The Cece Mystery: Next Steps
1. Search Cece's apartment for clues.

2. Brainstorm passcodes for her dad's phone.
3. Search for more clues at Opal's house.

I was trying to connect the dots, when the front door creaked open. I hopped off my bed and poked my head into the hallway.

"Hello?"

"LouLou girl! Just who I was looking for." James. I let out my breath. He must've worked the lunch shift.

I met him in the living room.

"Hi! You're home," I said.

"I'm home," James said. "And I was hoping you'd be here, too."

"Me? Why?"

"I have a message to relay," James said. "Your dad called me this morning. Said he'd been trying to get in touch with your mama, but she hadn't called him back."

I wasn't surprised. Mom was horrible at returning messages. Dad almost always called James instead.

"Oh, he did?" Even though this wasn't unusual, something about Dad talking to James made my palms sweaty. Like walking into a room when everyone goes silent, and you're pretty sure they'd been talking about you. I wasn't sure I wanted to know what James and my dad had talked about.

"He's off for a while starting on the sixteenth. He's hoping you can come to Kansas City that weekend."

I dug my heels into the carpet like it was mud.

I hadn't talked to Dad since I left Kansas City after my two-week last summer.

Something about that visit had been different. I didn't

feel different, but it was like he saw me that way. Just like with everyone else in my life lately, I couldn't figure out where I fit with him either.

My first clue was that he called me Lou. Just Lou. He used to call me Loulee or Princess Louise as often as he called me Lou.

The second clue was Chuck E. Cheese. There's one near his apartment, and we went there every time I visited. I know that Chuck E. Cheese is kind of dumb, and I'm too old for it, but it had been our place.

During this visit, we went to the wood-fired pizza place around the corner instead. It had white tablecloths and dim lighting. Dad didn't know what to do with his hands when we were there. He kept folding and unfolding his napkin. I ordered a Sprite, but there were no free refills, so I sipped it slowly.

"What's new at home?" he'd asked.

"Everything's pretty much the same."

Dad folded his napkin and set it on the table.

"Mom tried growing tomatoes in the backyard, but it was a total fail."

"Black thumb, huh?"

Dad unfolded the napkin and set it back on his lap. I sipped my Sprite.

"So what are you into these days?" he asked.

"The same stuff."

It was like we were meeting for the first time.

"This food is taking forever. How long does it take to cook a pizza?" He put the napkin on the table.

I sipped my Sprite and counted the bricks on the pizza

oven until finally our waitress appeared and plopped a large pepperoni on our table.

Then on my last night there, we went out for ice cream. Right before it was our turn to order, the teenager working behind the counter scooped the last bit of rocky road for the person in front of us.

Dad lurched forward.

"Are you going to refill the rocky road? You've gotta have more in the back, right?"

Rocky road is my favorite. At least it was. At home, I'd been ordering cookie dough all summer, but I hadn't told Dad that.

"Uh, no sir. We don't replace the flavors this close to closing." The teenager looked nervous.

"That's okay," I said. "I'll get something else."

"It's not okay. If you have more in the back, please go get it." Dad's voice rose.

"Sir—"

"My daughter's been waiting in line for rocky road, so I don't care how close to closing time it is."

My face was on fire.

"Dad, let's go." I grabbed his arm and pulled him away from the counter.

"Good idea," he shouted. "We'll take our business elsewhere."

Once we were outside, Dad turned to me like nothing had happened. His voice was at a normal level again.

"Should we try Dairy Queen? A rocky road Blizzard would be good."

"That's okay," I said.

"A different ice cream shop then?"

"I want to go home," I whispered.

"What was that?"

"I said, I want to go home!" I yelled, and I wasn't even sure why. Dad looked stunned. I wanted to take the words back as soon as I said them. I wanted to tell him that what I meant was I wanted to go to his apartment. But I didn't. And then we barely said two words to each other before I left the next day.

When I got to Mayfield, I'd wanted to tell Francie all about it. But she'd immediately bombarded me with stories about Tommy and the municipal pool. How Tommy and Braden had lain their towels next to hers, even though their usual spot was by the diving boards. How Tommy had asked her to play gutter ball, even though they'd never asked girls before. How he'd given her the second half of his Slurpee, claiming it was too sweet to finish.

So instead of telling her about Dad, I promised I'd spend every day until school started with her, at the Mayfield Municipal Pool.

"What do you think, LouLou girl?" James took out his phone and pulled me back into the conversation. My heels still dug into the carpet. "Want to call him back?"

"I don't think that weekend will work," I said.

"Why's that?"

"I'm super busy. We have this big project due. I'll need to be here. To make sure I'm ready."

It wasn't a lie. If we didn't hear from Angel soon, we'd

be working until the last minute. And scrambling to finish the essay sounded better than a weekend of my dad wiping sweat from his forehead, shoving his hands in his pockets, and struggling to start a conversation.

"Alright. But you need to call him back. And sooner rather than later, okay?"

James walked toward the hallway, but as he was about to head to his bedroom, he turned around and came back toward the couch instead.

"I know it's not my business. And I know your dad isn't perfect. But kiddo, nobody is. Sometimes you have to give people a few chances. And a little grace."

James was talking about Dad. But maybe he was talking about Francie, too. My face got prickly and hot.

"You're right. It's not your business."

The words jumped out of my mouth. As soon as they were out, I wished I could shove them back in.

James seemed to be thinking about what to say next. Before he could say anything, though, Tripp burst through the door, Lady Rainbow in one hand and his water bottle in the other.

"Daddy!"

He flew into James's arms.

Mom was right behind him, juggling Orla and her work bag.

"We had hot dogs and beans at school today. And you know what, Daddy?"

"What, buddy?"

"Beans are *not* a magical fruit."

James chuckled. "Oh, is that so?"

Mom set Orla on the floor, and she toddled over and grabbed James's leg.

"You're home early. I thought you were working a double tonight," Mom said.

"I got cut early. Last Thursday was super slow, so they figured tonight would be, too."

I hoped he wouldn't give Mom the message from my dad. At least not yet. She'd make me call Dad back right there on the spot.

It was like James could read my mind.

"I volunteered to be first cut, because I had a message to give Lou, but I'll let her share it with you. I was just going to shower."

"No, you're not." Tripp said this like it was a simple fact. "We are playing Magic Kingdom. I'm going to wear the purple cape because purple is my favorite color. And you are going to wear the blue cape with the stars on it, because blue is your favorite color."

"We are, are we?" James shrugged his shoulders.

Mom smiled. "You're welcome to take the dinner shift here then. I was planning on mac and cheese."

"With hot dogs?" He grinned and winked at me.

I forgot I was annoyed with James and laughed out loud.

"You two!" Mom swatted the air as if she would've swatted one of us if we were standing closer. "We can't all be world-class chefs, now can we? Make the mac and cheese any way you want. Better yet, make *anything* you want."

"I think it would be in everyone's best interest if I take you up on that."

It felt good to watch Mom and James, to be far away from Cece and Francie, to not have to think about Dad's message. The sweaty palms and prickly feeling slipped away.

18

THIRD GRADE

One Monday morning in third grade, our teacher Sister Genevieve announced a "special event." Our Lady of Perpetual Help was holding its first annual Donuts with Dad the following Friday.

I felt sick. I wasn't the only kid at school with a stepdad. But I was the only one with a real dad she barely saw. I knew if I gave the flyer to James, he'd come. It just wasn't the same.

At lunch that day, Francie and I sat in our spot, next to each other with our cafeteria trays touching. Madison Brewer plopped her pink lunch sack across from us. Her lunch sack was covered in tiny daisies. It had her name sewn across the front. She'd been sitting with us more and more lately, and usually we did our best to ignore her.

It's not that we hated Madison or anything. It's just that Madison tried so hard. She sucked up to the teachers, especially the nuns. She joined every after-school activity. And she laughed the loudest at everything Francie said.

Madison waved her hand in our faces. She bent her fingers toward us, so we could see her brightly painted nails.

"Do you like this color? Me and my mom got matching manicures this weekend."

I didn't know what a manicure was, but Sister Genevieve was teaching us how to make inferences. I inferred that it meant paying someone to do something you could do yourself.

"It looks like someone threw up cherry Kool-Aid on your hand." Francie smiled like what she said was a compliment.

Madison forced out a laugh.

"You're so funny, Francie. It's called Fire Engine Red."

"I like Kool-Aid Vomit better." Francie took a bite of her cafeteria pizza.

This time Madison ignored her.

"So, Donuts with Dad sounds fun."

"I guess," I said. I picked at my sandwich.

"They better get the donuts from Ms. Nettie, otherwise I'm not going." Francie took another big bite of pizza.

"Oh Lou, what was I thinking?" Madison covered her mouth with one of her hands and its Fire Engine Red nails. "Will your dad even be able to come? I didn't mean to leave you out."

"Oh, I don't know. Maybe. Or my—"

Francie broke in. "That's none of your beeswax, Madison."

"All I meant was it must be so hard not to have a dad. I mean not to have a dad that lives here."

I wanted to run from the table.

"Donuts with Dad is a dumb idea, if you ask me,"

Francie said. She nudged my shoe with hers under the table. "Who wants to come to school even earlier than we already have to?"

"I think it's a nice idea. I know my dad will be excited," Madison said.

Francie's shoe still touched mine.

"You would think something like that sounds fun, Madison."

Madison's mouth hung open.

"But we're not interested, and we had something we wanted to talk about. Alone." Francie waved her hand like she was shooing away a bug.

Madison's eyes got big, like Francie had kicked her, but she took her daisy lunchbox and moved to the other end of the table.

"You didn't have to do that," I said.

"Do what?" Francie grinned and took another huge bite out of her pizza.

~

Later at recess, Francie and I sat under the rusty slide.

"When we grow up, we should move far away from Mayfield," Francie announced.

"Totally," I agreed. "There are too many Madisons in Mayfield. We should move to New York. Or Arizona. It's always summertime in Arizona."

"We'll get an apartment together," Francie said. "And you'll get a smart job like a lawyer or a writer. And I'll be your assistant. I don't think you have to be smart to be someone's assistant. Oh! Or maybe you'll be a spy. And I'll be the only one who knows your secret identity."

I wanted to tell Francie that she was smart enough to get any kind of job she wanted. Maybe she'd be the one to grow up to be a real-life spy. She always thought of the best ideas anyway.

But I didn't.

Instead I nodded along and let her plan our faraway life. A life where we'd know so many people that Madison Brewer would be a distant memory.

~

On Tuesday morning, Sister Genevieve handed out a new flyer. This one announced that Donuts with Dad would now be called Donuts with a Special Grown-Up. I didn't know if Francie had anything to do with it. But on Monday, she had run back inside after school to "tell Sister something real quick." It might not have been her. It just seemed like something Francie would do.

19

Cece invited me to sleep over at her apartment on Friday night. I figured since we still hadn't heard from Angel, this would be a good chance to work on finding Cece's mom. I wanted to go over my ideas and get started. Plus, I was grateful for weekend plans.

In the coatroom, I had overheard Francie and Madison discussing what to wear to the Mayfield High football game that night. I buried my face in the row of backpacks and counted backward until they were gone.

Nannie arrived at our house as I was packing after school. She was watching Tripp and Orla while Mom went out for Mexican food and margaritas with her best friend Katy. James was working the dinner shift, like he always did on Friday nights.

Cece's dad would be home, so tonight wouldn't be our opportunity to search their apartment for clues, but maybe we'd be able to do some internet research or make a few phone calls. I scribbled a quick list in my notebook.

Potential Contacts
1. Aunt Julie
2. Other relatives? Friends? Neighbors?
3. Places she goes a lot—maybe they've seen her or could relay a message

"Louise, sweetheart, are you ready?" Nannie called from the living room. "Your mama's still getting ready, so I'm going to drive you to your friend's house."

I shoved my notebook in my backpack on top of my pajama pants and pulled my old sleeping bag out of the closet. When I dragged my stuff into the family room, Tripp was lying on the floor doing a puzzle. Orla toddled over to him, grabbed a puzzle piece, and stuck it in her mouth. He threw his hands up.

"This is hopeless!" He messed up all the pieces. "I'm coming with you. I want to see Francie." He popped off the floor and headed toward the door.

"I'm not going to Francie's, buddy."

"Why not?" He looked at me expectantly. I felt Nannie's eyes on me, too, like she wanted to ask the same question.

"Because. I'm going to a new friend's tonight."

"What's her name? Does she like Trolls?" Tripp had a huge collection of Trolls dolls. Every time Francie came over, she spent a good ten minutes playing them with Tripp.

"Her name is Cece. And I don't know, buddy. I'll ask her."

"I don't like her." He sat with his puzzle like he was going to give it another go.

Nannie swooped Orla into her arms.

"We're going to take this one with us. She's causing too much trouble." She winked at Tripp. "I'll be back before your mama leaves. I can't wait to see the finished product."

Orla patted Nannie's cheeks, and her smooth, brown hands contrasted against Nannie's pale wrinkles.

Nannie wrestled Orla into her car seat as I plopped into the front. I hoped we could make the short drive downtown without Nannie asking a bunch of questions. The way she looked at me when Tripp asked about Francie made me pretty certain that wouldn't be the case.

"A new friend, huh? Your mama tells me she's Opal Duncan's granddaughter."

Nannie nearly ran over the mailbox as she peeled out of the driveway. She's a terrible driver.

"Yep."

I stared out the window, hoping Nannie would focus on the road. No such luck.

"What about Francie? Your Friday nights used to be exclusively reserved for her."

"She went to the football game."

"Is she acting grown now? Is that the problem? Last time I saw her I wanted to wipe that makeup off her face."

"I don't know, Nannie. She's just going to the football game."

This was the longest car ride I'd ever taken.

"People change. But that doesn't mean you have to. You know that, right?"

I hoped this wasn't going to morph into some cheesy talk about growing up.

"I know."

Nannie rolled through the stop sign at the corner of First and Market. She made a U-turn in the middle of the street and parked outside Able & Payne.

"That's enough about that, then. We're here. Have fun and be good. That Duncan girl may be going through some things of her own."

"What do you mean?" What did Nannie know? What had she heard?

Nannie studied me. Then she chose her words carefully, something she never does. "I just mean because she's new, starting school a few weeks in, and all."

That wasn't what she meant, but I filed it away. I'd press her later.

Cece was sitting on the curb outside Able & Payne with a book in her lap. She popped up as soon as I closed the car door. I wished Cece's red ponytail was Francie's white-blonde one, but I pushed that feeling away.

"You brought the phone, right?" she asked as soon as Nannie pulled away.

"Yep. It's in my bag."

I had Mom's old laptop, too. Cece had no technology of her own, and we were going to need the internet if we stood any chance of tracking her mom.

"I thought you'd never get here. Being in there with him is driving me nuts."

My stomach fluttered. Maybe this wasn't a good idea. Mr. Duncan didn't *seem* dangerous, but now I wasn't so sure. I patted the pocket of my backpack that held the cell phone. I was glad I had it.

Cece led me through the door and up the narrow stairway.

Cece's dad looked up from the table when the door opened.

"Lou, welcome back!" He had a smile plastered to his face, but behind it his face was worn out. The bags under his eyes were even heavier and darker than last time. "Should we order some takeout? Chinese? There's a place around the corner."

"Come on, Lou," Cece said.

She turned down the hallway that led to her bedroom without looking at her dad. He stared after her. I stayed where I was, waiting to see which one of them would make the next move.

"Suit yourself," Mr. Duncan said. "I guess more for me and Lou, then. And if memory serves, this place makes a mean sweet and sour chicken. Have you had Ling's, Lou?"

"Yes. It's my nannie's favorite. We have it whenever we spend the night at her house."

"Your nannie has good taste. It's been around since I was in high school."

As her dad talked, Cece inched along the wall back toward the kitchen.

"Okay, fine. I'll have sweet and sour chicken. But only because I'm starving." She stood in the doorway.

"Good decision." Mr. Duncan took out his phone.

"Thanks, Mr. Duncan," I said. "I love their sweet and sour chicken, too."

He smiled and then went back to his phone. I studied his face, trying to figure out if there was something sinister

I was missing. He definitely looked exhausted. Maybe the guilt was keeping him awake at night.

"Lou, come on," Cece said. I followed her.

Cece threw my sleeping bag into the corner and grabbed her notebook off her desk. I sat on the floor and pulled my notebook out of my backpack.

"I came up with some ideas," I said, flipping to the page where I made my lists. "For how to find your mom. I mean, help your mom find you, I guess."

Cece jumped off her bed and settled on the floor next to me. I moved the notebook in front of her and she stared at the pages for longer than it should've taken her to read them. Finally, she looked up.

"I've been looking for signs everywhere. I thought I might feel something by being at Angel's. I kept expecting the universe to come through in some way. And I thought it hadn't. But I was wrong. You and your notebook are my sign. The universe brought us together."

"Does that mean you think my ideas might work?"

Cece's talk about signs and the universe still weirded me out, but I wanted her to be right anyway. I wanted her to be glad she asked for my help. And more than that, I wanted to be a good friend.

"Yes. They have to," Cece said. She smiled and looked at the lists again. "This is no surprise, really. Capricorns and Scorpios make a great team."

I fought the urge to count backward, and instead, I prayed that I could be the person, and friend, Cece believed I was.

20

We started with Aunt Julie. The name Julie Clark is about as common as Elizabeth Clark, and Cece knew frustratingly few details about Aunt Julie's life. Including whether she lived in Denver or Colorado Springs. She did know that she was a teacher, but... "She teaches middle school. Eighth-grade English. Or is it seventh grade?" And that she had a boyfriend, but... "His name is Leo. Wait, no, I think it's Theo."

Needless to say, when the apartment door squeaked open, and Mr. Duncan called, "Food's here!" we both welcomed the break.

It seemed like we were allowed to eat in Cece's bedroom, though I doubted she asked for permission. Cece ate her sweet and sour chicken and egg rolls with chopsticks. I dug around inside the bag until I found a plastic fork. We were stuffed to the brim and shoving the empty cartons back into the plastic bag, when Mr. Duncan called to us again.

"They put the fortune cookies in my bag. They're out here if you want them."

Cece didn't answer.

"Come on, Cee. I know they're your favorite."

Cece didn't move.

"I'll grab them," I offered.

Cece sighed dramatically, but she stood. "That's okay. I'll go. You know, most of the time fortune cookies are a flop, but every now and then there's a sign in one."

When Cece got back to the room, she'd already torn the plastic wrapper off her cookie. She tossed the other to me where I sat on the floor.

My fortune was in the flop category: *"Learn to stop procrastinating. Tomorrow."*

I could tell that Cece's wasn't a flop because a smile played at the corners of her mouth. She read the tiny strip of paper to herself several times before she read it out loud.

"In the end, all things will be known." She went to her desk and grabbed clear tape out of the top drawer. "I should've known better than to rush the universe."

Then Cece grabbed her notebook from her bed. She opened the front cover and carefully taped her fortune inside. I didn't interrupt. Cece took her place next to me on the floor.

"Where were we? Should we move on from Aunt Julie?"

"For now. Any other relatives? Close neighbors?"

"My mom's only family is Aunt Julie. Their parents died before I was born. We could try my neighbor Mrs. Jankowski. We talked across the fence sometimes. She has the most beautiful garden and makes amazing cookies."

"Oh, that's a good one. If your mom is back in Columbia, Mrs. Jankowski could give her a message," I said. "And we can track her down since her last name is less common."

I wrote *Mrs. Jankowski* in my notebook.

"What about your mom's friends? Or work? Where does she work?"

In my head, I listed who I would call if I were trying to find Mom. Her best friend Katy, who was practically like my aunt, her book club, her work friends. I was certain they'd know how to help me.

"She's talkative and social like a typical Gemini, but for some reason, she's never had many close friends. That must come from her moon sign."

Cece paused, like she was deciding if she should say the next part.

"She lost her job last year. She used to work at the university, too. It was really hard for her. And I don't know what happened, but she never found another job. My mom isn't like a lot of other moms. Me and my dad are all she has. She needs me. That's why we have to find her, Lou."

Cece had that breakable look again, and I knew I had the power to keep her together or shatter her into a million pieces.

"Mrs. Jankowski is perfect. Let's start there," I said.

I got Mom's old phone and laptop out of my bag. I flipped the screen open, and the laptop automatically connected to Able & Payne's Wi-Fi. I'd done my homework at Mom's office enough that the password was saved. I typed "Jankowski, Columbia, Missouri" into the search bar, and a short list popped up.

"Is her first name Jane?" I asked.

Cece knelt behind me, reading over my shoulder.

"Yes! That's her. Jane Jankowski on West Fourteenth Street!"

It only took me two more clicks to find a number.

"Let's call," Cece whispered.

I pulled the phone out and set it between us. The dialing pad filled the screen.

"Wait, what are you going to say?" I asked. This was important. Maybe we weren't prepared.

"I'm going to act casual. I don't think she needs to know what's going on. At least not yet. I don't want my dad to get in trouble."

We both knelt over the phone as Cece typed in the digits. It rang twice. Then a woman's voice.

"Hello?"

"Hi, Mrs. Jankowski?" Cece sounded about five years younger. "It's me. Cece. Cece Clark-Duncan."

"Cece! Oh my goodness. Are you okay?"

"Yes. Yes, I'm fine."

"Oh good. You scared me! I've been thinking about you. How is everything in . . . where . . ."

"Mayfield," Cece supplied. "It's okay. But that's not

why I'm calling." She took a deep breath. "I was wondering if you . . . if you'd seen my mother?"

"Your mother? Isn't she with you? I thought there was some kind of family emergency."

"Oh, yes. She . . . she went back to the house to get some stuff and she forgot her phone, so I wanted to tell her not to forget my favorite sweater."

Cece's eyes got wide. I gave her a thumbs up.

"Your favorite sweater? I see. I'm looking out the window now, and the house still looks empty, but I'll keep an eye out for her."

"Great. Thanks, Mrs. Jankowski. It was nice to talk to you." Cece clicked "end" before Mrs. Jankowski could respond.

Cece took another deep breath and stared at me like she was waiting for my feedback.

"Okay, now we know your mom's not there," I said.

"She's not there," Cece repeated. She shrank into herself.

"No. I guess not. But it was weird that she thought your mom was with you. Like your dad was trying to cover something up. And if your mom isn't at home, that means she's somewhere else. Looking for you."

"You're right." Cece sat a little straighter. "That was weird. If my dad has been telling me the truth, why would he need to lie to Mrs. Jankowski?"

"Exactly." I grabbed my notebook.

At the top of a new page I wrote:

Mrs. Jankowski: thought Cece's mom was in Mayfield (weird!), hasn't seen her, but will give her a message if she does.

"But do you think the other part is true? That she hasn't been there?" Cece asked. She picked at her fingernails.

"Maybe. Maybe she went back to Colorado when she realized you were gone."

"Maybe." Cece nodded slowly. "That has to be right. Aunt Julie is an Aries, so she'd be good at helping in a crisis."

"Let's keep trying to find Aunt Julie, then. But is there anyone else we should check with in Columbia? To make sure your mom hasn't been there?"

We were hitting a dead end, but I didn't want Cece to know that. There had to be a clue somewhere that we could use.

"She went to this coffee shop near our house every day," Cece offered. "I went there with her a few times, and one of the guys that worked there knew her name and her order."

"Okay. Let's try it." It was worth a shot.

"It's called Albatross and it's on Elm Street."

I typed "Albatross Coffee, Columbia, Missouri," and quickly found a sleek website for a modern-looking shop. As Cece keyed in the phone number, I heard footsteps in the hallway. They got closer. Cece either didn't hear it, or pretended not to, because she went right on typing the number.

Two rings. "Albatross Coffee. How can I help you?" The footsteps stopped right outside Cece's door.

"I'm looking for a customer of yours. I've misplaced her number, and I'm hoping you might be able to pass on a message."

The door to Cece's bedroom opened. Cece didn't look up.

"Her name is Elizabeth Clark. She has dark red hair. She always orders an almond milk latte with one pump of vanilla and an extra shot of espresso."

Mr. Duncan stood in the doorway. Cece pretended he wasn't there. I made myself as still as a statue. I willed the floor to open and swallow me whole.

The voice on the phone was overwhelmingly loud. "I'm not sure. But I haven't been in in a few days. Hold on. Let me ask someone else."

"Cece, what are you doing?" Mr. Duncan looked at the phone and then the open laptop. *Albatross Coffee— Columbia, MO* blared across the screen like a giant neon sign advertising our plan.

"Are you still there?" The voice from the phone.

"Yes, I'm here." Cece never once looked up, even as Mr. Duncan walked over to the phone and tapped "end."

"Cece, what are you doing?"

"It's none of your business." Cece's voice was younger again, the way it was when she spoke to Mrs. Jankowski.

Thirty. Twenty-nine. Twenty-eight. I wanted to get out of there. I knew I shouldn't be listening to this conversation. Mr. Duncan didn't say anything, but he didn't move either. Cece filled the emptiness.

"I'm looking for help. So Mom will know where I am. You'll be happy to know that thanks to you, we didn't get anywhere." The hard edge returned to her voice.

"Cece..." Mr. Duncan took a deep breath.

"Mom would never choose to be away from me. I know you're lying." Cece balled her fists around the edge of her shirt sleeves. She clenched her jaw to hold back tears. I knew what she was doing because I'd done that, too, about a million times.

Mr. Duncan rubbed his eyes. His shoulders sagged.

"Cece, sweetheart. Maybe now is not the time to be having this conversation."

He meant because I was sitting right there. I scrunched into the corner and made myself as small as possible.

"I should go . . . I'll call my mom," I said quietly.

"No! You don't need to go anywhere. Lou can hear anything she wants."

Mr. Duncan took another breath.

"Cece, I don't pretend to know what your mother's plan is. What I do know is that she could be here if she wanted to. This isn't easy for me either."

Cece flinched like he'd slapped her.

"You're a liar! You're doing this to get back at her because she wanted to separate. It's like you hate her! You know what? I hate *you*!"

Now Mr. Duncan was the one who looked like he'd been slapped. His cheeks flushed, and I swear, his eyes filled with tears.

"Cece, please. I know you're angry."

"Get out." Cece spat the words. "I mean it. Get. Out."

Mr. Duncan rubbed his face.

"I think we need to take a break before we talk about this. No more phone calls, please."

Cece didn't answer, but she slid the phone toward me, surrendering it.

Mr. Duncan slowly backed out of the room and shut the door behind him.

Cece turned to me. Her face was tomato red and her voice was soft again. "Don't believe him. My mom would never do this. My mom loves me."

21

When I got home from Cece's on Saturday, I spent most of the day trying to make sense of what happened the night before. I couldn't shake that in-over-my-head feeling. But then, the not-wanting-to-let-Cece-down feeling hit even harder, and I was stuck. I sorted the thoughts racing around my head in my notebook.

The Cece Mystery: What I learned at the Cece Sleepover

- Her mom isn't in Columbia—at least not at their house. Where else could she be? Colorado? Brainstorm more possibilities.

- Her dad lied to Mrs. Jankowski.

- Her dad said her mom could be here if she wanted to, but a kidnapper would say that to convince Cece (and me?) that he didn't do anything wrong.

- Nannie knows something (or thinks she knows something). She would not have let me spend the night there if what she knows is that Mr. Duncan is a kidnapper.

- Conclusion: We have more work to do.

On Monday at school, Cece didn't mention the sleepover and I wasn't about to bring it up. Instead, we forged ahead. Cece said she would keep working on a way to contact Aunt Julie, and I decided we needed to search the apartment for clues as soon as her dad was away.

And Angel finally got back to us.

Cece and Lou,

I'm available for the project interview on Friday afternoon. I'd like to include a free reading, as it's an important aspect of my business that you should see firsthand. If you are still willing to help with advertising, I have a stack of flyers I'd like hung on bulletin boards around town. The library, the community center, and Nettie's all have one. I'll leave them in my mailbox.

Be well,

Angel

We decided to help with the flyers on Tuesday after school. Cece was giddy about the free readings. I was still skeptical about astrology and the universe and signs, but my curiosity was growing.

"This is exactly what we needed!" We'd just picked up the flyers and were trudging toward the library. "I *hoped* she'd do a free reading, but I wasn't sure, you know? And now, it's all happening on Friday!"

"What exactly is happening?" I was afraid Cece's hopes were too high.

"I'm getting answers." She said it simply, like I should have come to that conclusion on my own.

"But what if—"

"There are no what-ifs, Lou. Don't you see? The universe

brought us to her. And now I'm going to know. I'm going to know how and when my mom will find me."

I wanted to say that sometimes things do just happen, and the universe has nothing to do with it. I didn't think the universe made me say the terrible, horrible things. That was a decision I made on my own. I believed that if the universe had its way, I'd have my best friend and Cece would have her mother. Saying that wouldn't be especially helpful, so instead I read Angel's flyer.

Angel Sweeney

Astrologist and Card Reader

Discover the YOU you've always been and the PATH you are meant to follow.

Astrology and Card Readings starting at $25

Find ME and I'll help you find YOU.

I shivered, even though it was still hot outside. Cece couldn't stop smiling. I didn't know if the universe and God were one and the same, so I covered both bases: I prayed once to God and once to the universe that somehow, some way, both Cece and I would find the paths we were meant to follow. The path that would lead Cece back to her mother and the one that would lead me back to Francie.

~

Cece and I made the rounds. Any place in Mayfield that had a spot for advertising, we found it. We hung Angel's flyers at the library, at Nettie's, at the community center, at the Baptist church, at Tripp and Orla's daycare, and even in the back of the chapel at Our Lady of Perpetual Help, though I was certain that Father Fred would tear it right down.

We were headed back to Angel's with the leftover flyers when I remembered one last place.

"There's a corkboard in the lobby of Able & Payne," I said.

"Oh, right. Above the newspaper dispensers?"

"Exactly. My mom keeps it organized, so she can make sure it doesn't get covered or taken down or anything."

"Perfect. And then I'd be home. My feet are killing me."

We turned onto First Street. Maybe Cece's dad would be out running errands, I thought. But as we got closer to Cece's apartment, I saw his white car was parked out front.

We pulled the heavy doors open. I spotted Mom behind her computer, so I went to her desk and explained what we were doing. Cece stayed in the lobby looking for the most eye-catching spot to hang the flyer. She secured it squarely in the middle of the board.

"I'll make sure the flyer stays front and center," Mom promised.

When I came back out, Cece had opened the newspaper dispenser. She grabbed a copy of the *Mayfield Gazette* and sat cross-legged on the floor.

"What's up?" I asked.

"Aren't you curious to see what Angel writes in her column?"

The *Mayfield Gazette* came out once a week and was dominated by high school sports stories, updates from the town council, and recaps of town traditions, like the Christmas tree lighting and the River Days festival. It was delivered to our house each week, but I never saw anyone read it. Mom used it to cover my books at the beginning of each school year and James used it as a fire starter through the winter. James reads the news on his iPad and Mom listens to a bajillion podcasts, so I guessed they got enough that way. Besides, anyone could figure out what's going on in Mayfield just by spending a Saturday morning at Nettie's.

I didn't know there were horoscopes in the *Gazette* until I met Cece.

"We can see how good she really is," Cece continued.

I sat on the floor next to her. "Sure."

"Just so you know, the horoscopes in the newspaper are like a watered-down version of astrology," Cece said. She handed me the paper. "They only talk about your sun sign."

I read mine out loud.

"Forgive yourself first. Release the need to replay a negative situation over and over again in your mind. Don't become hostage to your past by reliving your mistakes. Release it and let go."

Thirty. Twenty-nine. Twenty-eight.

Act normal. I couldn't let Cece see how much Angel's words spooked me, how accurate they were.

Cece wasn't paying attention to me. She read her own horoscope.

"The path ahead will become clear, and what once felt like a battle you'd never get through will become a story about how it all worked out. You'll be glad you never gave up when you see the way things are about to align for you."

Cece was as light and happy as I'd ever seen her.

"Lou, this is *it*. I knew we were on the right track. I can't wait for Friday."

Cece's enthusiasm sucked me in, and my doubt about Angel began to fade. There was no denying the words were eerily relevant. Maybe Cece was right. Maybe the answers were right there. We just needed a guide to help us find them.

As Cece folded the paper and shoved it into her messenger bag, the door that led to her apartment opened. Mr. Duncan stepped into the lobby.

He took a step back when he noticed us sitting on the floor.

"Whoa, what are you two doing here?"

Cece stood and dusted off her uniform skirt. "We were working on our school project, but we're done now. We're leaving. Right, Lou?"

Cece gestured with her eyes toward the doors that led outside. I knew she wanted to get out of there, but something else occurred to me.

"It's nice to see you again, Mr. Duncan."

Cece shot me a look. I gestured toward the stairs with my eyes and hoped she got my message.

"Where are you headed?" I asked.

"I told Cece's grandmother I'd grab something she needs at the grocery store so she doesn't have to go out again. Want to come, Cee?"

Cece's eyes met mine, and I knew she understood.

"That's okay. I'll stay here and get going on my homework." She smiled, and I was pretty sure it was the first time I'd seen her smile at her dad. I hoped he wouldn't get suspicious.

He hesitated, like he was considering forcing her to come along, but then he nodded. "Okay. I'll be quick. Shouldn't take more than a half hour or so."

"Take your time. I'm sure Grandma will love the company." Cece smiled again.

I silently willed her to say something rude to make her behavior more normal, but Mr. Duncan didn't ask any questions. He waved and walked out the door.

I scurried toward the stairs, and Cece came after me. We were through the door and in Mr. Duncan's bedroom in less than ten seconds.

A neatly made queen-sized bed sat in the middle of the room under the window. A small chest of drawers and a desk took up one corner. The walls were empty, and so were the tops of the dresser and desk. Two half-full boxes sat on the floor next to the desk.

"We left a lot of our stuff in Columbia," Cece said. "My dad said he didn't know how long we'd be here, but that he wanted to be close to family while he figured it out."

I nodded.

"Or maybe that's a lie, too, and we're never going back. Who knows?"

"He must be planning to go back sometime." I opened the closet door. "I don't think he'll be able to make do for long with just these clothes."

Two collared shirts, a pair of pants, and a jacket hung in the closet. A small suitcase was shoved in the back corner.

"Why don't you look through the desk and dresser, and I'll check out those boxes," I suggested. The boxes were out in plain sight. The more private stuff should be Cece's job.

Cece pulled a dresser drawer open, and I knelt on the floor next to the boxes.

I rifled through the first one. Reports and textbooks, probably for his job at the university.

The second box was more of the same. I was about to tell Cece I'd go check out the living room, when my hand touched something glossy. A photograph? I pulled it out. A postcard. Snow-capped mountains against a clear blue sky. *Colorado Springs, Colorado* was printed across the bottom.

On the back, Cece's name was written in loopy script. And under her name, an address. West 14th Street, Columbia, Missouri. Her old house.

My darling Cece,

I miss you! Aunt Julie's is fun (but not as fun as being with you).

I'll see you soon, and I can't wait!

Love you (times infinity!!) Mom

I reread it five times, studying every word of Cece's mother's jagged cursive. What was the postcard doing in this box? Why hadn't Mr. Duncan given it to Cece? How could he let her think her mom wasn't trying to get in touch?

Fifteen. Fourteen. Thirteen.

"Let's go over what we know," Cece said.

It was Wednesday, and we sat cross-legged at the back of the school yard against the chain-link fence.

When I had shown the postcard to Cece yesterday in Mr. Duncan's room, she'd traced her mother's words with her finger. She blinked back tears and took it to her room without saying a word. I had followed after her, not wanting to get caught in her dad's room alone. I watched from the doorway as she buried the postcard in the top drawer of her dresser. When she turned around, her eyes were clear, and she smiled. But not her real smile. It was the smile of someone trying her best to seem normal.

"My dad will be back soon, so you should probably go downstairs. I'll make sure his room is clean," she'd said.

I hadn't pressed her. I followed her instructions and figured she'd bring up the postcard when she was ready.

Cece was ready as soon as we got to school Wednesday

morning. She passed me a note during Dr. Morgan's morning prayer and announcements.

we need to figure out what the postcard means. ASAP. Lunch?

From where we sat at the back of the yard, we could see what everyone else was doing. Most of the boys were playing touch football. Madison and Annabelle were under the rusty slide. They were far enough away that they couldn't hear us. Plus Francie wasn't there, so that made it more bearable. Francie had homework detention. She'd only ever turned in her homework some of the time, but lately it was none of the time. Mrs. Jackson made a new rule that if you didn't turn in homework, you had to stay inside with Sister Margaret and finish it. I suspected Sister Margaret gave Francie candy and plenty of attention.

The postcard sat on the grass between Cece and me. Next to it, my notebook was opened to a new page, where I'd written *What We Know About Cece's Postcard* across the top.

"My dad hid it from me. Even though it was clearly *for me*," Cece said.

"Right. Very suspicious."

1. Cece's dad hid the postcard—suspicious.

"And it's obvious that your mom thinks she'll be seeing you soon," I added.

"Totally."

2. Cece's mom thinks they'll see each other soon.

The postcard did not make Mr. Duncan look good, but something about it had tugged at the corners of my brain since I'd first read it. I'd tried to remember every word of it as I lay in bed last night, every detail, but nothing I remembered cleared up the nagging uneasiness.

Now I picked it up and turned it over in my hand. I reread it. I studied where Cece's mom had written her address.

And then, as if it was asking me to notice, the postmark seemed to light up.

Just above Cece's address, the postcard was stamped with the date and location from which it was mailed. September 30. Kansas City, Missouri.

My face was hot and I stared at the stamp until it turned into a blurry blob of ink. Her mom mailed the postcard on September 30—just a week ago. And not from Aunt Julie's house in Colorado, but from Kansas City.

She was only a couple hours away.

I placed the postcard back between us.

"Did you notice this?" I pointed at the postmark.

Cece stared at it, and I stared at her. I didn't know how she would react, or even what I thought it meant, but I braced myself anyway.

"I can't believe I didn't notice it before. This is unreal, Lou. She's in Kansas City because that's where she thinks *we* are. She's looking for me there." A chunk of hair slipped out of Cece's messy ponytail, and she shoved it behind her ear. "We've been there tons of times, and it's a bigger city, so she must've thought my dad would try to hide me there."

I honestly had no clue if that's what it meant, but Cece was convinced and I needed more time to think. So, I added to the list:

3. Cece's mom is in Kansas City looking for her.

The postcard confused me. Cece had been in Mayfield for almost five weeks—as of a week ago, her Mom didn't know she was missing? And why would she send it from Kansas City pretending to be in Colorado?

But her dad *had* hid the postcard from her, and that was weird, too. It was possible that Cece was exactly right, that her mom was searching for her somewhere it seemed way more likely her dad would go.

By the end of lunch period, we had added:

4. Could the message be some kind of code?

When Mrs. Jackson blew the whistle, I closed my notebook, Cece shoved the postcard in the pocket of her uniform sweater, and we both brushed grass off our skirts.

"I can't believe she's so close," Cece said. We walked toward the line forming at the school doors. She stopped suddenly and spun toward me. "I'm going to dinner tonight at my grandmother's house. Maybe you could come with me? It will be awful, but better if you're there."

Opal Duncan had scared me *before* I knew she might be involved in a kidnapping, and my experience at her house hadn't made me less afraid. But we were making headway, and Cece wanted, maybe even *needed* my help.

"Of course. I'm sure my mom won't mind."

"Awesome."

Then something occurred to me. "Maybe there are more clues in her house. If she lets us out of her sight, we need to look around."

Cece grinned and patted the postcard in her pocket. "What would I do without you, Lou?"

A warm glow buzzed through me. It was the opposite

of the heart-pounding, river-roaring-in-my-ears, counting-backward feeling. We had to solve this mystery.

Mrs. Jackson led our class into the building and down the hall toward our classroom. When we walked by the main office, Francie was waiting by the open door, math book in hand.

"See you later, Sister Margaret, probably tomorrow." Francie laughed like homework detention was a joke. "Thanks for the lollipops!"

Then she joined our line, right behind Cece and me. She slipped the math book under her arm and dug around in her skirt pocket, eventually pulling out a tube of lip gloss—bubble-gum pink and sparkly. She put a thick coat on her lips, then held the tube out to Cece.

"Want some?"

I held my breath waiting to see what Cece would do.

"Thanks, but I'm good." Cece pulled her ponytail tighter and kept her eyes focused ahead.

I exhaled and walked so close to Cece that our shoulders touched.

23

FOURTH GRADE

In fourth grade, I got knocked out of the school-wide spelling bee on the word parallel. *As long as I live, I won't forget that set of double ls again.*

The spelling bee is for fourth through eighth graders, with two representatives from each class. Kyle Rodriguez and I were the fourth graders, and no one expected either of us to win, so I tried to feel good about making it to the fifth round. That was two rounds longer than Kyle and three rounds longer than both fifth graders.

After my double l mistake on parallel, I joined the others who'd been knocked out in a row of folding chairs on the left side of the stage. One by one our row grew bigger, until Francie's sister Bernie won the whole thing.

Her winning word was environment.

"E-n-v-i-r-o-n-m-e-n-t," she said. Her voice and body language exuded confidence. She flipped her blonde hair over her shoulder and smacked her glossy lips together on the last letter.

"That's correct," Dr. Morgan said.

Byron Petty, who was the runner-up, had his fingers crossed at his sides. He held his head in his hands when Dr. Morgan proclaimed, "And the winner of this year's Our Lady of Perpetual Help All-School Spelling Bee is Mary Bernadette Fitzpatrick!"

Francie flew out of her seat. She whooped and clapped and yelled, "That's my sister!" Then she waved at me where I sat with the other contestants on the side of the stage. I felt proud of my association to both of them.

Afterward, there was a reception in the church social room for contestants and their families. Everyone else had to go back to class.

Both of Francie's parents were there, which was unusual. I tried to think of another school function I'd seen her mom at, and I couldn't. Her dad came to some stuff but always alone. I guess that made it extra special that Bernie won the whole thing. And I knew Francie loved any excuse to get out of class. Mr. and Mrs. Fitzpatrick, Bernie, Francie, and their little sister Tess sat around a round table in the corner of the room. Bernie was talking loudly and gesturing wildly, and the rest of the family had their eyes fixed on her.

James was working the lunch shift, so it was just me and Mom. We grabbed our cookies and watery punch and settled into seats at a table near the Fitzpatricks'.

"Honey girl, I am just so proud of you." Mom took a bite of cookie and checked her watch.

"I can't believe I forgot the second l," I said.

"That word will stick with you now, that's the good news!" She looked at her watch again. "The bad news is I have to get back to work. I have a meeting that I promised I'd be back for, and it starts in ten minutes. Will you be okay if I go?"

I glanced over at Francie's table where she was laughing with her mouth wide-open. Probably at something Bernie said.

"Sure. I'm good."

Mom gave me a tight hug, and then left. I moved my chair next to Francie.

"Welcome to the winner's table!" she said.

"And just think. I have two more years to defend my crown." Bernie pulled out a tube of pink, sparkly lip gloss and slathered it on her lips. "How did I look onstage?"

"Like an angel," Mrs. Fitzpatrick said. She spoke about two levels softer than her daughters. "We're so proud of you."

"Brains and beauty, what can I say?" Bernie smacked her lips together like she had onstage.

"Give me that." Francie grabbed the tube of lip gloss off the table and smeared it on her own lips. "If I can't have brains, at least I can have beauty! How does this look?" She turned toward her mother.

I wanted to tell her it looked ridiculous, like some kind of clown princess. But she wasn't asking me.

"Good, dear," Mrs. Fitzpatrick said absently. She reached across the table and pulled Bernie's trophy in front of her. "Environment is really a tough word."

24

I reminded myself to be extra polite at Opal Duncan's house. She clearly valued manners and if she liked me, she'd never suspect I was there to snoop around.

I'd watched her closely last Sunday at Mass. I even took some notes in my notebook, in case I noticed something important that might help me help Cece.

Opal Duncan: Seems serious about church. Closes her eyes a lot. Shushed the Rodriguez boys and scooched away. Has a lot to pray about? Is she worried about something? Asking for forgiveness?

I figured a lot of grown-ups were serious at Mass, so that by itself wasn't necessarily the sign of a guilty conscience. But I couldn't rule it out either.

Mom agreed to dinner without any trouble. She rummaged around the cabinets and found a scented candle to give to Mrs. Duncan. She said it would be rude to come empty-handed. She valued manners, too. We were running late as usual, but by six o'clock, she loaded Tripp and Orla into the car, and we headed to Opal Duncan's gravel road.

Mr. Duncan's little white car was parked out front when we pulled up, and Cece answered the door.

"Lou! Thank the Lord, you're here. I cannot deal with those two for another second."

She gestured toward the hallway. Mr. Duncan and Opal were in the formal living room sitting in straight-back chairs that looked uncomfortable. I didn't understand the point of rooms like that.

Cece walked past her dad and grandmother without looking in their direction—the same way she'd avoided eye contact when Opal picked us up from school.

"Cecelia. Stop right there. Please allow us to properly greet your friend."

Cece kept walking.

"Cee." Mr. Duncan's voice was a warning.

"I see your manners are still atrocious. I said stop where you are. Hello, Louise. It's nice to see you again," Opal said.

Cece rolled her eyes, but she stopped and turned toward her grandmother.

"It's nice to see you again, too." I held out Mom's candle. "Thanks for having me."

Opal smiled. "It's a pleasure to have you back in my home. Thank you for this lovely gift. I'm glad Cecelia is making friends." Her smile faded, and she turned back to Cece. "Although it's difficult to see how, with that attitude and those manners."

"Mom. That's unnecessary," Mr. Duncan cut in.

"It's the truth. Is it not?" Mrs. Duncan shrugged her shoulders.

"I said that's enough, Mom. And Cece, let's be a little more respectful, okay?"

"We're going outside. Come on, Lou." Cece stomped past her grandmother. She stomped past me. She stomped into the kitchen. And she flung open the door that led to the backyard.

"Thanks again." I waved awkwardly before I scampered after Cece.

Once the door slammed shut behind us, I relaxed.

"Can you see now why my dad hated living here? Why his childhood was horrible?" Cece said.

"She scares me, that's for sure," I agreed.

Cece led the way to a bench in the middle of the yard. We could see across the open land all the way to where the sky hugged the earth.

"Do you think there's any way we'll be able to look around?" I asked. "Or do you think it's too risky?"

I wanted to get back on Opal's computer, but that didn't seem likely with her and Mr. Duncan sitting in the next room. We still hadn't figured out why they had the power of attorney document. Cece remained convinced it was proof her dad and Opal had attempted this before. We also needed to follow this Kansas City lead, but I wasn't sure we'd be able to accomplish much under Opal's watchful eye.

"I know she's going to come out here any minute and ask me to set the table. She always does. So, we could look around in the kitchen? She might get suspicious if we try to go upstairs. I never go upstairs," Cece said.

"The kitchen works. Let's start there."

As if on cue, Opal Duncan popped her head out from the back door.

"Cecelia, would you and your friend set the table, please? Dinner will be ready soon."

Cece stood and headed for the door.

The kitchen smelled like onions. The heat outside, coupled with whatever was in the oven, made the air hang thick and heavy.

Mrs. Duncan watched us for a few seconds, but when Cece started bustling around in the silverware drawer, she rejoined Mr. Duncan in the living room. A pocket door opened to another room where the dining table sat. Cece took her time setting the table while I tiptoed around, looking on the countertops and opening drawers.

Each drawer and cabinet held exactly what it should—cooking utensils, casserole dishes, mixing bowls.

"The table's almost ready. We just need one more minute," Cece called into the living room, more for my benefit than her dad and grandmother's.

That's when I saw it. A small book like the one Nannie used to keep track of her friends' addresses and phone numbers. I knew we couldn't get the book out of there, so I riffled through it instead. Maybe I'd find a number we could use—Aunt Julie, or better yet, Elizabeth Clark herself. A slip of paper fluttered to the floor and I snatched it up.

MCI to ORD 10/18 1:00 ORD to SFO 10/18 3:10

Feet shuffled toward the dining room. Without thinking, I shoved the paper in my pocket.

"The table looks lovely. Thank you, Cecelia." Through

the pocket door, I saw Mrs. Duncan pull her chair out at the head of the table. I scurried to take my seat.

The meal was about as comfortable as our meeting in the living room. Cece only spoke when her grandmother asked a direct question. Even then, she gave one-word answers.

"Anything new or interesting at school?" Mrs. Duncan asked.

"No."

"What are you learning about?"

"Nothing."

"I see you're as sullen as usual. Would you like to talk about it?"

"Nope."

"I'm sure Louise didn't join us to watch you give me and your father the silent treatment."

Cece shrugged.

The chair dug into my back. The casserole on my plate reminded me of something Nannie would make, but even its comforting smell couldn't cure the uneasy feeling in my stomach. I wanted Mom's mac and cheese, hot dogs and all.

"Cee, we're trying our best here," Mr. Duncan said. "Maybe Lou wants to tell us what's going on at school." The bags under his eyes sagged. He rubbed the stubble on his chin.

Cece rolled her eyes. Mrs. Duncan saw it and let her fork fall. It clattered on her plate.

"Cecelia. That is enough. It is not your father's fault, or mine for that matter, that your mother is not here. We know you're hurt by her choices, but it is time you stopped taking it out on us."

Cece leapt out of her chair with so much force that the chair toppled to the ground.

"Shut up! Just shut up!" she screamed. "You're both liars!"

"Cecelia! That is—"

But Cece didn't let her grandmother finish. "We found the power of attorney. And we found the postcard. We know Mom's looking for me, and we know this isn't the first time you've tried this. Right, Lou?"

I froze. Fork in midair.

"Cece. Honey." Mr. Duncan rubbed his eyes. "I was going to show you the postcard. In fact, I looked for it last night and couldn't find it. And that document, how did you even—"

Opal cut in. "If by 'this isn't the first time' you mean this isn't the first time your mother has disappeared for weeks on end, then you're right. This isn't the first time. Then and now, your father and I had to make sure you'd have proper care."

Cece's fists were clenched, and her whole body shook.

"I said, SHUT. UP."

She ran through the dining room, into the kitchen, and out the back door.

I looked from Cece's dad to her grandmother and back again. Neither looked at me.

"Did you need to do that tonight?" Mr. Duncan rubbed his temples.

Mrs. Duncan stabbed her casserole. "I've had it with

the lack of respect, Aaron, and I think it's time you quit dancing around the truth with her."

"Not everything is as black and white as you seem to think it is, Mom."

It was like I wasn't even in the room, so I slowly slid my chair back and followed Cece outside.

I scanned the yard, and at first, I didn't see her. I moved my gaze further. Her black Converse poked out from the side of a shed at the back of the yard. I found her sitting with her back against the wall, knees to chest, head in hands. When she looked up, her face was tear-streaked.

"I hate her," Cece said. "She's a liar."

I sat next to Cece. I wrapped my arms around my knees, too, and didn't say anything.

"Her explanation didn't even make sense. I think I'd know if that happened. They'd both say anything to keep me from her." Cece balled her hands into fists and wiped at the tears streaming down her cheeks. "You believe me, right? My mother would not *choose* to be away from me like this."

I struggled to make sense of what I knew so far. What Opal had said. What Cece told me. The growing list of clues in my notebook.

One thing was clear. Cece hurt. And she needed a friend.

I nodded my head. "Of course, I believe you."

25

I couldn't shake what Mrs. Duncan had said about Cece's mother. Even after Mom picked me up and asked me a million questions: "What did you eat?" "Did Mrs. Duncan like the candle?" "What did you talk about?" Even after we got home, and Orla crawled into my lap and Tripp asked me a million questions of his own: "Why does music have sound?" "Why is ice cold?" "Why do cookies bake in the oven?" Even after I went to my room and blocked it all out with my math homework.

And then there was the slip of paper in my pocket. It probably had nothing to do with Cece or her mother. Nannie's address book was stuffed with random notes and scraps where she'd scribbled someone's new address or a random message while she talked on the phone. I'm sure Opal Duncan did the same thing.

My brain couldn't rest without investigating what it might mean, though. I got out of bed and opened the old laptop. I grabbed the scrap from where I'd stuck it inside the front cover of my notebook.

MCI to ORD 10/18 1:00 *ORD to SFO* 10/18 3:10

I typed *MCI* into the search bar. The first result was a link to Kansas City International Airport. That was weird. What did those letters have to do with the airport? Under that there were several businesses with MCI in the title. Nothing connected to Cece.

Next I tried *ORD*. The first link was to Chicago O'Hare International Airport. Two airports. Maybe the codes were abbreviations for the airports? I'd only been on an airplane once, when we went to Mom's cousin's wedding in Florida two years ago. We'd driven to Kansas City and flown from there.

When I tried the whole thing—*MCI to ORD 10/18 1:00,* a bunch of links to flight information from Kansas City to Chicago popped up.

A travel plan. I'd cracked the code, and the answer wasn't helpful. It was probably for a trip Opal was planning, or left over from a trip she'd already taken. I'd ask Cece what she knew about this, but I was sure it was another dead end.

~

The next day was Thursday. The second Thursday of the month. Confession Thursday.

Every second Thursday, Mrs. Jackson walked us from class over to the church building across the street. Nobody ever whispered or fidgeted or goofed around. When we got there, Father Fred led us in a series of prayers while I scoured my brain for a sin worthy enough to confess but not bad enough to raise Father Fred's eyebrows.

One by one, we sat in front of Father Fred and shared our sins. It was terrifying. Father Fred whispered prayers and then assigned us our penance. It was usually to say a few Hail Marys while we waited for the rest of the class to finish. And then—almost as bad as confessing—we had to recite the Act of Contrition from memory.

I never forgot the words, but Francie said she did once and Father Fred stared at her until she remembered them. She said it was a true act of God that the words came back to her. Francie confessed fighting with her sisters every time.

This second Thursday was like all the others, except this time, when I searched my brain for sins, I kept coming back to the same one. The terrible, horrible things I couldn't unsay. But there was no way I could confess that. It would make them too real.

Cece wrung her hands next to me. This was her first confession at Our Lady of Perpetual Help. Maybe it was her first confession ever.

Right before Father Fred started his prayers, and just as I decided this month's sin would be talking back to Mom, the church doors swung open. The Daughters of Isabella poured through. Sixth grade shared their confession time with the church's women's group. The Daughters of Isabella met every Thursday morning for Bible study, church activity planning, and—according to Nannie, who was the secretary—gossip. On the second Thursday of the month, they went to confession, too.

I'd never noticed that Opal Duncan was a member. She was in the middle of the group, but I spotted her white bun and her tight expression right away.

Nannie led the pack. Typical.

"Louise! Ready to make that conscience crystal clear?" Nannie called out to me across the church. If only.

Tommy and Braden snickered. I gave Nannie a small wave and a look that I hoped told her to tone it down.

"Nannie, hi!" Francie popped out of her pew. Nannie had told Francie to call her Nannie the first time they'd met, and Francie loved it.

"Mary Frances Fitzpatrick! Knock me over with a feather." Nannie stood next to Francie's pew. She stuck her arms out for a hug, and Francie went in. My heart hurt.

"It's good to see you, honey." Nannie pulled away and looked Francie up and down. Then in a loud whisper, Nannie said, "Does your teacher let you roll your skirt that high? I thought this school had rules." She winked at Francie to let her know she was kidding. But I was sure Francie knew that Nannie half meant it.

The Daughters of Isabella took their seats in pews across the aisle from us. Nannie and her friends got to make their confessions to Father Ray, the assistant pastor, behind the safety of the confessional screen. Us kids had to go face-to-face with Father Fred up on the altar.

Somewhere between trying to figure out what I was about to confess and trying not to forget the words to the Act of Contrition, an idea occurred to me. I knew from experience that the girls' bathroom was on the other side of the wall from the confessional. When the bathroom was empty and you were in the furthest stall, you could hear everything. What if Opal Duncan confessed what she'd done to Cece? Surely adults used confession to *actually* clear their consciences.

I didn't dare risk whispering my idea to Cece. I'd have to wait until my turn passed, ask Mrs. Jackson to go to the bathroom, and hope I timed it right to catch Opal's confession.

Clinton Mulvaney was ahead of me, and he took forever. Maybe he forgot the Act of Contrition. I shivered and repeated it to myself one more time to be safe.

I made it through my turn, but my hands shook the whole time.

Father Fred barely had time to say, "I absolve you of your sins in the name of the Father, Son, and Holy Spirit," before I was out of the chair and off the altar.

"Mrs. Jackson, can I use the restroom?" I crouched next to where she sat at the end of the last pew and whispered. "It's an emergency."

Mrs. Jackson nodded. I assessed the pews filled with the Daughters of Isabella. Someone from the second row was in the confessional, and Opal Duncan sat in the third. It would be her turn soon.

I pushed my way into the church lobby. I expected it to be empty, so I startled when I realized there was someone else in there. A woman. Her back was to me, and she was leaving. Before I had time to register much, she was gone. The heavy doors swung shut behind her.

I didn't think I recognized her, but this was tiny Mayfield, so that didn't seem possible. And I hadn't seen her face. Just a dark jacket and a dark red ponytail. She'd tightened it before she pushed through the doors.

26

It bothered me that I couldn't place the woman. But she was probably just leaving the adoration chapel or helping with something in the social room. I was sure it would click into place, and I was on a mission.

The bathroom was empty, and I went into the far stall. I could make out voices without pressing my ear to the wall, but once I did, I could make out words.

Father Ray powered through the women's confessions. It turned out they weren't so different from us kids. Of the three I heard, none were remotely juicy. They confessed "speaking ill of a neighbor," "losing my temper with my grandson," and "snapping at my husband." One of them even forgot the Act of Contrition. Father Ray didn't wait for her to remember—he said it for her.

None was Opal Duncan.

Our class would finish soon, and if I didn't come back out, Mrs. Jackson would send someone in to find me.

I almost gave up, when a prim and gravelly voice wafted through the wall. Opal Duncan.

"Bless me Father for I have sinned. It has been four weeks since my last confession."

I pressed my ear tighter against the wall. The voice on the other side started again as the bathroom door opened and several sets of feet trotted in.

I was so close, I could've melted into the wall. But it was no use. The voices in the bathroom drowned out the voice from the confessional.

"I don't really need to use the bathroom, I wanted to check my hair." It was Madison.

I peeked through the space between the stall door and the floor. Next to Madison's pink Nikes were Francie's red slip-ons and Annabelle's loafers.

"How does that look?" I imagined Madison turning her head from side to side as she let Francie and Annabelle check her ponytail for bumps.

It was impossible to hear through the wall now. Another dead end.

"Can you believe how messy Cece's ponytail always is? Maybe we should offer to help her."

Annabelle lowered her voice to a loud whisper. "Madison. It's because she, like, doesn't have a mom."

"Does she not have a brush?"

I wanted to slam the steel door open and slap Madison across the face, but the growing pit in my stomach told me to stay in place.

"It's so sad," Annabelle went on as if Madison hadn't said anything. "I heard that her mom, like, totally abandoned her. Vanished without a trace. My mom told Mrs. Maguire that Cece's mom has *issues*."

The pit in my stomach grew. *Fifteen. Fourteen. Thirteen.*

"That's dumb, and you're being dumb for repeating it." Francie. "Whatever is going on with her mom is none of your business. And I like Cece's style. I think she makes her ponytail messy on purpose, and it's cute on her." Francie's feet moved to leave.

"Francie!" Annabelle called after her. "I was just saying what I *heard*."

"What if people were going around repeating everything they *heard* about your mom. Would you want that?"

The bathroom door swung open and then shut. Madison's and Annabelle's feet scampered out after Francie's.

I sat there, alone and confused. Was Annabelle right? And if so, how did it connect with the dinner at Opal Duncan's? How did it connect with Cece and her shoebox full of clues? None of it made sense.

What's worse, I got this weird pang of jealousy hearing Francie defend Cece. I hated myself for it.

And then there was Mrs. Fitzpatrick. I knew better than anyone why Francie hated how the other girls spoke about Cece's mother. She knew how it felt. I'd spent countless days and nights at Francie's house and only spoken to her mom a handful of times. I saw her at Sunday Mass, but never at school events. In second grade when I asked Francie where her mom was, she answered with a sharp edge in her voice. "I don't know. Probably praying. Or sleeping." It was clear I should never ask again. And I never did. I mentally made a list in my head: *Reasons I'm the World's Worst Friend*. I added this to it.

It made sense that Francie was angry about what Annabelle said. She felt some kind of connection to Cece that I could never understand. I was sick to my stomach and I didn't even get what I'd wanted in the first place—Opal Duncan's confession.

By the time I left the bathroom, my class had already crossed the street and was entering the school building. So much for Mrs. Jackson noticing I was missing.

As I waited to cross, a silver car pulled out of the church parking lot. I was sure the driver was the woman from the church lobby—I could make out the dark jacket and ponytail. As she drove by, she pushed her sunglasses off her face. And like the final piece of a giant jigsaw fitting into place, my brain clicked with recognition. It was the woman from Cece's shoebox of clues.

Her mother.

27

FOURTH GRADE

*I discovered the thin wall to the confessional in fourth grade.
Right after the annual Christmas performance.*

A special part of the fourth grade at Our Lady of Perpetual Help was that performance. The fourth graders acted out the Nativity scene. As each grade took turns performing a Christmas song, we stayed on stage, in character but frozen likes statues. The songs were Baby Jesus–focused, of course. "O Holy Night," "Hark! The Herald Angels Sing"—that kind of thing.

Then after the eighth graders finished their song, the Nativity scene came alive and performed the Christmas story as the grand finale. The whole thing ended with what was supposed to be a moving rendition of "Silent Night."

An excited energy descended on our class right after Halloween. We couldn't wait to find out what roles we would play. Sister Angeline, our teacher, was young and new to the convent and by extension, the school. That must've been why *she picked Francie to play the Virgin Mary. If she'd been at Our Lady of Perpetual Help longer, she would've known better.*

I played the donkey. The donkey had no lines, and its only job was to stand behind Mary and then walk across the stage with her to the inn and then back to the stable.

It was embarrassing, but Francie made it bearable.

During rehearsals, she added lines about the donkey— "Poor, pregnant me could never make it to Bethlehem without my sweet and very pretty donkey!" "It's a good thing I have the world's best donkey to keep me safe in that God-awful stable!" "Thank you for the frankincense! Did you bring anything for my donkey?"

I threw in a few "hee haws!" here and there, too, to make Francie giggle.

Sister Angeline was a nun, but not strict. Every time Francie invented a line, she raised her hand, like she was waiting for Francie to call on her, and said, "Mary Frances, can you please stick to the script?"

I'm sure Sister Angeline really regretted her decision on the day Francie asked about adding a birth scene.

We'd gotten to the part in the story where the lights dimmed and Clinton Mulvaney, who played one of the shepherds, grabbed the doll wrapped in swaddling clothes from backstage and placed it in the manger.

Francie leapt to her feet from where she knelt on stage.

"Sister!"

"Yes, Mary Frances?"

"What if we did a live action birth scene? You know, really surprise the audience? Make it realistic? I could do all

that heavy breathing and screaming and stuff, and my donkey here could be like a birth coach!"

The whole class laughed.

"That would be awesome!" Tommy shouted from backstage. He was one of the Three Wise Men—the one who brought the myrrh.

Sister Angeline's eyes widened, and she dropped her copy of the script.

"I don't think we should add scenes, Mary Frances."

"I'm only kidding, Sister. Don't worry! On the big day, I promise I'll stick to the script. I'll make you and the Virgin Mother proud."

The class laughed again, but I knew Francie wasn't joking.

When we weren't in front of the rest of the class at rehearsals, Francie was committed to her role. We practiced together every day after school until Francie had her lines memorized. I read the line and Francie repeated it back until she could've said the lines in her sleep.

"You're going to be awesome," I said. We were in Francie's room the day before the show. Francie was nervous, which wasn't normal for her.

"I know," she said. "But my mom's going to be there, and I want to be extra great for her." Francie cleared her throat. "She's, like, obsessed with the Virgin Mary, so it's the least I can do."

Mrs. Fitzpatrick had never been to a Christmas performance. In second grade, Francie sat with me and Mom and James while the nuns served cookies and punch in the cafeteria after the show. Her dad stood by the door with his hands shoved in his pockets. As soon as Francie finished her cookie, she ran over to him. Her sisters were right behind her, and the girls and Mr. Fitzpatrick left together. I wondered where Francie's mom was, but I never asked.

On the day of the show, we had to get there early, so Mom picked up Francie and dropped us off outside the school. The entire time we were in the car, and then backstage getting in our costumes, Francie never stopped talking. Francie always had a lot to say, but this time was different. It was like she wanted to fill the air until there was no room for anything but her endless chatter.

Finally, we took our places on stage, and for the first time all night, Francie fell silent. I knelt next to her, ridiculous in my brown sweatsuit and donkey ears.

"Hee haw! Break a leg!" I said in my best donkey voice. Francie stared straight ahead.

The curtain rose, and the kindergartners filed on stage. While they sang "Little Drummer Boy," I scanned the audience for Mom and James. It was hard to see faces through the blinding stage lights, but I could make out Mom's curls in the second row. When I glanced at Francie during first grade's "Away in a Manger," she was doing the same thing. I looked for her parents, too, but the auditorium was crowded, and everyone blurred together.

I was distracting myself from fifth grade's off-key rendition of "It Came Upon a Midnight Clear" when the auditorium door swung open, casting a stream of light down the center aisle.

Mr. Fitzpatrick slinked in and took a seat in the back row. He was alone.

I glanced at Francie. She still stared straight ahead, like she hadn't noticed. But her chin trembled, and I knew better.

"Maybe she's here," I whispered.

Francie ignored me.

She stayed like that, staring straight ahead, jaw clenched, through the rest of the songs.

Then, Annabelle, who was the narrator, said, "And it came to pass, that all the world should be taxed in the place of their birth. So, Joseph and Mary set out for Bethlehem."

This was our cue to walk across the stage toward Braden and his cardboard cutout inn.

Francie didn't move.

"Joseph and Mary set out for Bethlehem," Annabelle repeated.

Kyle Rodriquez, who was Joseph, grabbed Francie's sleeve and gave it a tug. I nudged her forward with my head. The audience laughed nervously.

A light switched on beneath Francie's blank stare, and she crossed the stage.

"No room!" Braden shouted, more aggressively than necessary. "You can sleep in the stable with the animals!"

"What do you mean there's no room? Can't you see I'm about to pop out a baby here?" Francie ripped the blue veil off her head and threw it on the ground at Braden's feet. "We're coming in! And you better have room service!" She stomped off stage.

Sister Angeline stood behind the curtain, her eyes wide. She grabbed the veil off the ground, pulled Madison out of the chorus, and shoved her next to Kyle in Francie's place. I crawled off stage after Francie.

I found Francie sitting against the wall in the hallway outside the auditorium. She had her knees pulled to her chest. Even her clenched jaw couldn't stop her chin from trembling.

I slid my back down the wall and sat cross-legged next to her.

"She said she was coming."

"Maybe there was an emergency."

"There was no emergency. She didn't care enough."

The first chords to "Silent Night" wafted out of the auditorium.

Francie sighed. "That was supposed to be my big moment."

I don't know what came over me. Maybe it was Madison standing where Francie should've been. Maybe it was seeing Francie so sad. Whatever it was, I spotted a fire alarm secured to the wall across from us and a streak of orneriness longer than Francie's passed through me. I got up and stood next to it.

"We don't have to let this become Madison's big moment, do we?"

Francie's jaw relaxed into a grin. Without saying a word, she popped up, and I pulled the lever.

Then we ran.

~

The next day at school, Sister Angeline made us go to confession as part of our punishment.

While we waited in our pew for Father Fred, I was so nervous that I excused myself to the restroom so I didn't throw up all over everything.

And that's how I discovered the paper-thin wall.

As I knelt by the toilet trying not to breathe through my

nose, Francie's voice floated into the stall. I pressed my ear to the wall.

"Bless me Father, for I have sinned. It has been, um, not that long, since my last confession. I'm going to confess and everything. But before I do, there's something you should know." She took a deep breath.

"What happened at the Christmas performance was completely, one hundred percent my fault. Lou Bennett is here, too, but she shouldn't be. I walked off stage, and I pulled the alarm. She was just trying to help."

I wanted to reach through that wall and wrap Francie in the tightest hug imaginable. I wanted to shout from the rooftops that I had the best friend in the entire world. I wanted to march right into the Fitzpatricks' house and tell Mrs. Fitzpatrick that she'd missed out on something special.

But I didn't. Instead, with my nausea melted away and a smile I couldn't shake, I went back to the pew and waited for Francie.

28

By the next morning, I had convinced myself there was no way the woman at church was actually Elizabeth Clark. The more details I tried to remember, the more I knew that I had to be wrong. I'd only seen Cece's mother on her shoebox, and I hadn't studied the pictures that carefully.

But in the unlikely case that it *was* her, then that could only mean one thing. She knew where Cece was. Maybe she was hatching an elaborate plan of her own. Maybe she was going to go to the Mayfield police. Maybe she already had.

It didn't help that Friday was full of bad news.

James figured out that I hadn't called Dad back because I never told Mom about the message. So James told Mom himself. She greeted me at breakfast with her phone in her outstretched hand.

"Call your dad and tell him you'll see him next week." She had that don't-you-dare-try-to-argue-with-me look.

But dumb old me tried the school project excuse anyway.

"It sounds like you'd better use your time wisely and turn that essay in before you leave town." When Mom's set on something, it's hard to make her see it another way.

And there was no part of me that wanted to tell her the real reason I didn't want to go. If she knew how badly the summer visit had gone, she'd say something to my dad, make me go to Kansas City anyway, and then the whole thing would become a million times more awkward.

So, I made the call. Dad answered on the second ring.

"Hi, Dad. It's me."

"Lou, hi. Did James tell you about next weekend? I'd love it if you could come."

"Yeah, he did. And I can. I mean, that sounds great."

"That's good."

We both paused.

"And hey, I'm gonna call that ice cream shop and make sure they're stocked with rocky road." He laughed nervously.

"You don't have to do that."

"I'm kidding, but I can. If you want."

"I'll see you next weekend, Dad."

Then we both hung up. I didn't feel any better.

~

I got the second piece of bad news at school.

Part of me hoped that Cece wouldn't be at school. That maybe her family had reunited and the whole big, sad mystery was solved, and in just the way that Cece wanted it to be.

But Cece popped out of her seat as soon as she saw me walk through the door.

"Lou! I got a message from Angel. She said thanks for the work we did for her. I guess our work was so good that she got several bookings right away. She has an appointment after school today, so she can't meet with us anymore. She asked if we could come on Tuesday instead."

No mention of her mother. And if Cece didn't know her mother had been in Mayfield, there was no way she'd actually been here. If I'm being honest, I was relieved.

"I guess that's okay," I said. "But maybe we can get some of it done this weekend."

"That's a good idea. We can write about the horoscopes and do that Catholic section we promised Mrs. Jackson. You can spend the night again, if you want."

"Okay. Cool," I said. "I need to have the whole thing done before next weekend. My dad is off work and he wants me to come to Kansas City. I'm trying to get out of it, but if I can't we need to finish by the time I go."

I hung my backpack and turned to walk to my desk. Cece stayed rooted right where she was.

"You're going to Kansas City?" Her eyes were big.

"Maybe. I don't want to, but we'll see."

"Why don't you want to go?" It hit me that she was thinking about the postcard. And her mom.

"I don't know. Last time I was there, it was weird."

Cece's eyes brightened.

"What if I went with you? Maybe if you have a friend there, it'd be less weird with your dad."

The word "friend" gave me that warm, glowy feeling.

Even Francie had never been to Kansas City with me. I suddenly loved this idea.

"And, what if my mom's still there and we could track her down?"

The dark-redheaded woman pulled at a corner of my brain. If it *was* Cece's mom, then her mom probably wasn't in Kansas City. But it couldn't have been her. I'd spent so much time thinking about Cece and her family that my mind must've been playing tricks on me.

"I'll ask my dad, but I don't think he'll mind." I turned out of the coatroom and tried to push away the nagging feeling that something wasn't right.

Francie walked toward us. She brushed by me, but she smiled at Cece. "Thanks again for letting Braden have it the other day. He's the worst."

"The absolute worst," Cece said.

"I like your shoes." Francie passed Cece and went to hang her own backpack.

Cece smiled. Cece's shoes were black Converse high-tops. My shoes were plain white tennis shoes from Walmart. Mom bought me the same pair every year before school started. I'd never hated them until now.

~

Mom was more excited than I was about another sleepover.

"You and Cece have gotten pretty close." She sat on my bed watching me pack my backpack.

"I guess so."

"I think it's great!" She was too enthusiastic. "Cece can use a friend right now."

"What do you mean?" It shouldn't have surprised me

164

that Mom might know something about Cece and her family, except that she'd never mentioned it before. I hadn't had a chance to ask Nannie about it either, so maybe now was my chance to find out what they knew.

"I'm sure she's going through a lot, trying to make sense of her . . . situation."

The way Mom said *situation* made me think she'd heard the same rumors Annabelle spilled in the bathroom. The idea of the whole town talking about Cece made me sick to my stomach. I decided to skip my chance.

"Can we talk about something else?"

"Okay. Sure. How's Francie? Is she going to this sleepover too?" Now my stomach churned.

"She's not. And, we're not really friends anymore. So, I wouldn't know how she's doing."

"Whoa, what? Not friends anymore? But the two of you—"

I knew Mom would want an explanation about what had gone wrong between us. I knew she was about to pepper me with a million questions. Maybe Mom was the one person who could help me figure out how to fix it. But I was too ashamed to ever confess the terrible, horrible things. I couldn't stand it if Mom knew how awful I was.

"Things change," I said.

"That's true. You know I want to help, right? Nothing you could tell me would ever change what I think about you."

It was like she could read my mind. She was the first person who assumed that I might share blame for what happened. That it wasn't all Francie's fault.

I wanted to curl up in her arms like I was five. I wanted her to rub my back while I told her everything. I wanted to tell her that I'd hurt Francie, and I didn't think I could ever fix it. I wanted to tell her that I was desperate to help Cece, but I didn't know if that was possible.

"I know," I said instead. I zipped my backpack. "I'm ready to go."

~

Cece was waiting on the curb again when we pulled up.

I double-checked my backpack for the old cell phone, the laptop, and my notebook before I opened the car door.

I let Mom kiss me on the cheek, and then I hopped out and joined Cece on the sidewalk.

We went through the Able & Payne lobby and up the narrow staircase.

"My dad went to get some pizzas." Cece opened the door to the apartment. "He's starting to ease up on leaving me home alone."

She led me down the hall to her bedroom.

"Should we get started on the essay?" I grabbed the laptop out of my bag.

"Sure," Cece said. "Don't you think it's incredible that we found Angel? Maybe she can tell us if Kansas City is the right place to look for my mom."

I didn't want to talk about Angel and whether or not she could read into our futures. I wanted to get back to what I was comfortable with—facts, dates, evidence.

"We can use her website to write the section about her background and then fill in any gaps later," I said.

I flipped the laptop open and typed in Angel's website address. I rummaged through my backpack. I forgot a school notebook, so I pulled out my leather-bound notebook instead. When I opened the notebook, the scrap of paper I'd found at Opal's fluttered out onto the bed.

"What's this?" Cece asked.

"I meant to ask you about that. It fell out of your grandmother's address book at her house." I smoothed the scrap and laid it on the laptop's keyboard. "I looked it up and I think it's a travel plan. This is information for a flight from Kansas City to Chicago. Has your grandmother been to Chicago? Or is she planning a trip?"

"Not that I know of. But I guess I wouldn't know." Cece grabbed the paper and studied it. "How'd you figure that out? About the flight, I mean?"

"It was easy." I typed *MCI to ORD* into the search bar.

The same information popped up. Cece leaned in to get a closer look. She studied the paper again.

"Lou, this flight is for next week. Next Sunday. The paper says *10/18*."

Now, I leaned in, too.

"My grandmother is not going to Chicago next weekend. She's running the quilting booth at the Daughters of Isabella craft fair."

"Whose flight could it be?"

"What's the other set of letters? Did you search those, too?"

I hadn't. Once I cracked the code, I brushed it off as a dead end.

I searched *SFO*—the airport code I hadn't looked up the first time. *Homepage | San Francisco International Airport* appeared.

"California," Cece whispered.

I held my breath and typed *ORD to SFO*.

Sure enough. Links to flight information for trips from Chicago to San Francisco. The second leg of the trip.

"Our trip." Cece pulled her knees to her chest. "This is our trip. I knew it. She booked it."

Cece rocked back and forth. I inched closer to the screen.

"It's worse than I thought," Cece said. "They must've known she had this planned. That's why my dad brought me here. That's why he kidnapped me. He was afraid that we might leave and never come back."

Cece's theory made sense. And it seemed more and more likely that Cece's theory was right. Her mom was in Kansas City. Whatever I saw—whatever I *thought* I saw—was wrong.

"Maybe she's still going to go. Or maybe she's hoping my dad will come to his senses and bring me home in time for the trip. Either way, we have to get to Kansas City."

My heart thudded in my chest, so loudly I was sure Cece could hear it. It was like the current of the river dragged me under as the weight of Cece's story pushed me further down. I struggled to the top and took a gulping breath. Cece's eyes were big, and round, and pleading with me.

"Please, Lou. We have to go to Kansas City."

I nodded. "I guess we do."

Cece wrapped me in a hug. "She's going to find me, Lou. And it's all because of you."

~

The reddish-orange light of early morning peeked through Cece's closed blinds. I was startled awake by a voice. Mr. Duncan. I could tell he was trying to keep his voice hushed, but his volume went up and down, like he was arguing with someone.

Cece lay perfectly still, curled into a ball with her back to me. By the even way her back moved up and down, I was certain she was asleep. I inched my sleeping bag closer to the door. If I lay still, I could hear what he said.

"I know you need time. But what about her?"

Long pause.

"You were in Mayfield and you didn't bother to see her?"

Another pause.

"You wanted to make sure she's okay? What's that supposed to mean? Of course she's okay. How long are you planning to be gone?" Mr. Duncan's voice was quiet but I felt his anger through the wall.

"Elizabeth?

"Oh for Christ's sake. Elizabeth?"

Then nothing.

29

That phone call replayed itself in my head over and over for the rest of the weekend. I decided to keep what I'd heard to myself. At least for now.

My notebook was the only thing that kept me from counting backward, that kept the river current from sucking me under.

What I Know:

1. The postcard—sent from Kansas City, but pretending it was from Colorado

2. The flights—Kansas City to San Francisco, the trip Cece said her mom planned for her

3. The woman at church—must have been Elizabeth Clark

4. The phone call—Cece's mom knows where she is and isn't planning to come back for her

What I Should Do:

1. Find a way to tell Cece about the phone call.

2. Convince Cece to talk to her dad.

3. Do NOT take Cece to Kansas City until you tell her the truth.

~

I walked into school on Monday morning convinced I knew what I was doing. Once the truth was out in the open, I'd be the friend that Cece needed me to be. This would bring us closer together. And once Francie saw what a supportive friend I was to Cece, she'd forget about the terrible, horrible things I'd said, and we could be a tight-knit threesome by Halloween.

I was an idiot. By lunch, my plan had completely unraveled.

"Lou!" Cece followed me into the coatroom as soon as I walked through the classroom door.

"Please tell me you talked to your dad about Kansas City, because I have everything all worked out. Mostly."

"Not yet." I hung my bag. "And, I think we should talk about that."

"Yes, definitely. There's a lot to figure out. The most important part is finding a way to get to the airport. That's why I'm so glad I have you, and why I'm so glad you're a Capricorn."

I gathered my thoughts and turned to face her. Cece's ponytail was messier than usual and her brown eyes were wild.

"What I mean is, I'm not sure we should go."

Her eyes narrowed. Her freckles did that thing where they almost popped off her face.

"What do you mean? How could we not? I *know* my

171

mom will go to the airport. She'll be hoping my dad will do the right thing and bring me back to her. That we'll go to California together, like we planned."

"Right. But about that," I started.

I stumbled to find the words that would do the least amount of damage. I didn't know what they were.

"Lou. You promised to help me. And you promised we'd go to Kansas City. I need you."

I chewed on my bottom lip. Cece had that fragile look. I knew that whatever I said next might break her.

Before I could speak, Francie burst into the coatroom.

"Cece! Just who I was looking for." Francie waved a pink envelope. Cece's name was written across the front in Francie's handwriting.

"This is for you." Francie thrust the envelope into Cece's hands. "It's an invitation for my birthday sleepover. I know it's kind of short notice. But I hope you can come. It's Saturday."

Francie stood next to me, but it was like I wasn't there. She jutted her shoulder out, blocking me from the conversation.

The roaring-river sound whirred through my ears. My heart sunk to my toes. *Thirty. Twenty-nine. Twenty-eight.* Before I could stop them, the words spilled out.

"We'll be out of town. Cece's coming with me to Kansas City this weekend to visit my dad."

Francie turned and looked at me like she just noticed I'd been standing there the whole time. Cece's eyes brightened and a huge smile stretched across her face.

"Right," Cece said. "Sorry to miss it, but we'll be in Kansas City."

Sweat sprung under the collar of my uniform shirt.

I hated myself for letting jealousy and anger keep me from doing what I knew was the right thing. Even though I knew I shouldn't, I kept going along with Cece's plan.

~

At lunch, I slipped into my usual spot and kept my head down while I unwrapped my turkey sandwich. Cece's tray clattered onto the table.

"Ugh. Apparently, our cafeteria hasn't heard of the healthy lunches movement. Look at this grease." Cece blotted her pizza with a napkin and kept talking. "That was random. About Francie and the birthday party, I mean. Do you know her sign? I'd guess Aries—they're super impulsive. But she's got to be a Libra or a Scorpio, based on the timing of the party."

"Her birthday is October twenty-third," I said.

"How'd you know that? I thought you weren't friends."

"We're not," I said quickly. "But I've known her since kindergarten. I know everyone's birthday by now."

"That makes sense. She's a Scorpio then. Barely. Sometimes when your birthday is close to another sign, you can share characteristics. She's bossy like a Scorpio. But everyone likes her like a Libra."

I tensed. The bite I'd taken out of my sandwich became Play-Doh in my mouth. I knew that if Cece kept getting to know Francie, she'd choose her over me, no question. Anyone would. I would, too.

"But don't worry. I would never go to her party. Even if we weren't going to Kansas City. Not if you weren't invited."

That should've made me happy. I swallowed the lump in my throat and changed the subject.

"I'll call my dad after school and make sure he's good with everything," I said.

"Great." Cece rubbed her hands together. "Let's get down to business. Any ideas on how we get to the airport?"

My heart wanted to be in this with her, but my head kept repeating the words from that phone call. *I know you need time. How long are you planning to be gone?*

"Maybe if we tell my dad we want to go somewhere alone, like shopping or something, he'll drop us off and we can get a cab. But that costs money." I had no money. I hoped Cece didn't either.

"That's not a bad plan. My dad has a bunch of cash in his sock drawer. I saw it when we were looking for clues."

"Are you sure? Maybe we should get the money another way." Cece was headed off the side of a cliff, and instead of reaching out to stop her, I was nudging her closer to the edge.

"We could also ask Angel. I know this is the direction the universe is pulling me, but she'll be able to tell us for sure. Maybe she'll have a vision of how our reunion is going to go," Cece said.

I wanted to pull her back from the cliff's edge. I wanted to tell her that I wasn't sure we could find her mother in Kansas City. That even if we did, her mother might not want to be found.

"Yeah, let's talk to Angel," I said instead.

✺ 30 ✺

Record-breaking heat covered Mayfield like a blanket. I never stopped sweating. The mess I'd gotten myself into with Cece made it hard enough to breathe as it was, without the humid air trying to suffocate me, too. My hair stuck to the back of my neck and thinking about that phone call and what I'd promised Cece only made it worse.

I knew I needed to talk to Cece, but I wasn't sure how. There was no easy way to tell her what I knew. Her dad had offered her the truth, and that hadn't ended well. She'd stopped talking to him and convinced herself he was a criminal. If that was easier than accepting the truth about her mom, how would things end for me?

I'd already lost Francie. I didn't want to lose Cece, too.

On Tuesday, we finally had our meeting with Angel. We planned to interview her for the essay and stay for the readings she promised us. Even if I didn't believe in astrology, I still wished for something to happen that would let me know what to do. I was running out of time.

"Do you have the list of questions?" Cece asked. We passed the bus line and headed toward the crosswalk.

"Yep." I reached around and patted my backpack.

"Let me do most of the talking. I think she can sense that the universe brought us together."

I nodded.

We walked for a block in silence. I tried and failed three times to tell Cece about the phone call. When we were close enough to Angel's that the fields at the municipal park came into view, I managed to push a question out into the air between us.

"Do you think your dad has talked to your mom at all? Since you've been gone, I mean?"

Cece tensed. "No. That would be impossible. He has a new number, remember?"

"Maybe he's called her, then?"

We passed two houses before Cece answered.

"Only if he was trying to throw her off. Convince her we're somewhere that we're not." We passed another house. "But I don't think so."

"Yeah, probably not." Maybe that *was* right. Maybe Mr. Duncan was trying to keep Cece's mom away. Maybe that's what they'd been talking about.

But in my gut I knew that wasn't what I heard.

"What time will we leave for Kansas City? Does your mom take you there? Or will your dad pick us up?"

"We usually meet him halfway, but sometimes I take the train. I still need to talk to him. Make sure it's okay if you come."

Cece stopped in the middle of the sidewalk.

"Wait. What? We're supposed to go on Friday."

"I'm sure he'll say yes. I've been avoiding calling him, is all."

"Lou! This is important!"

"I know it is," I said. "And I promise, I *swear*, I'll call him as soon as we're done here." We were back on the cliff's edge, and on my last chance to pull Cece away, I'd pushed her into the dark, swirling water instead.

She let out a deep breath, and her shoulders loosened. My heart ached.

~

Mercury's paws padded toward us before we even rang the bell, with Angel's feet right behind him. The door swung open. Today, Angel wore a long skirt and black tank top. Her bare arms were covered in tattoos I hadn't seen last time. There was a constellation and one that reminded me of the zodiac poster Cece had hanging on her wall.

"Ladies. Come in." She gestured toward the room where we'd sat before. Cece and I chose the same chairs. Angel sat on the couch and tucked her legs under her skirt. Mercury heaved himself next to her and nestled into the crook of her legs.

I dug into my backpack and pulled out my school notebook with the list of questions we wrote together. I held it out to Cece. She set it in her lap but didn't look at the list.

"We are so excited to learn more about you. And we are so, so thankful for this opportunity," Cece started. "Right, Lou?"

"So thankful," I repeated.

Cece tightened her ponytail and leaned in.

"I'm not sure your teacher will approve, but you might earn points for creativity," Angel said.

"At least it's not for a real grade," I added.

Cece shot me a look. I remembered what she said about letting her do the talking.

"Anyway. Let's start with a few questions about the services you provide through your readings." Cece pulled a pen out of her messenger bag.

"Go for it," Angel said.

"How accurate are you at predicting future events?" This question wasn't on our list, but Cece's determination told me not to interrupt.

"If my clients are truthful and provide me with information about their birth charts, then I'd say pretty accurate."

"Like how accurate? I'm looking for a percentage here."

"I don't always follow up with clients, so it's hard to say for sure." Angel looked from Cece to me and back to Cece. "I thought you wanted to know about my background?"

Cece shrugged. "The more information we have about, um, everything, the better. Are you able to explain people's past? Like why certain things have happened to them?"

"Yes. Again, based on the birth chart."

"And how accurate would you say you are with that? A percentage would be great if you have one." None of this was on the list.

"I don't have one."

"Okay. What about bad people? Can you help people figure out who in their life should not be trusted?"

Angel's eyebrows creased in the middle. They had crept up her forehead with each of Cece's questions.

"Cece, why don't we go back to the list?" I pointed to the notebook on her lap. I knew what Cece was doing. And I knew the essay wasn't what mattered to her. She was here for answers. Answers I had. "I think our first question was something like what's your favorite thing about your job?"

Cece glared at me, then sighed and looked at the list.

"Yes, that was it."

We spent the next fifteen minutes asking questions like "How did you get started in astrology?" and "What role do you think you play in making the community a better place?" We had plenty of material for the essay. We knew we weren't going to win, but we'd have something to turn in. I wanted to leave.

"I think that was our last question. Cece, are you ready?" I stood.

"Lou. The readings."

"Oh yeah," I said. I slid back into my chair and pretended I'd forgotten.

Angel studied Cece. There was a question in her eyes, but I couldn't read it. Cece locked eyes with Angel and didn't look away.

"Are you sure you wouldn't rather come back another day?" Angel asked.

"No! You said we'd do it today." Cece seemed like she was on the verge of tears.

"Okay. Of course. I thought you might be tired, that's all."

Cece straightened her back. "We're fine. And we're ready."

"Great. Then let's go ahead. I think I'll invite Lou back first."

My stomach flip-flopped.

"That's okay. Cece can go first." I didn't want to go at all, much less go first. I sat on my hands to keep her from noticing how badly they shook.

"I'd prefer you, Lou." Now the question in her eyes was for me.

Angel walked toward a door that led into a sun porch on the side of the house.

"It's fine, Lou. Go," Cece whispered. "And if the time is right, ask about Kansas City."

Thirty. Twenty-nine. Twenty-eight. I stood, grabbed my backpack, and followed Angel.

Two wicker chairs sat opposite each other on the porch. Between them was a small round table. An intricately engraved wooden box was on the table next to a deck of cards with images I didn't recognize. Angel gestured toward one of the chairs and I sat down. She closed the door to the porch before sitting in the second chair. She didn't waste any time.

"What's going on with Cece?"

I froze. "What do you mean?"

"I mean, why are you really here? The school project, sure. But I mean why are you *really* here? What's going on with Cece?"

Angel leaned forward. Her elbows rested on her knees. Her eyes were soft. It was like she knew what I was going to say before I even had to say it.

"I don't think I know what you're talking about."

I couldn't betray Cece's confidence, but I was trapped. I knew Cece wanted something from Angel, expected something from Angel. And Angel knew it, too.

"Lou, honey, I think we both know that's not the truth." Angel's voice was gentle. "I'm concerned. It's clear that Cece wants something from me, and I'm not sure I can provide that. Or that I should."

The understanding in Angel's eyes was like a pillow after a long day. And I was so tired.

Everything I'd gathered over the last few weeks—Cece's note, her shoebox, the postcard and the flight information, what Annabelle said, what Opal said, what Cece said, that phone call—snowballed into an avalanche.

"She thinks her dad kidnapped her. And she thinks you can help her find her mom."

My heart pounded in my chest. The river whirred through my ears. I wanted to count backward and get out of that room.

Angel heaved a sigh that moved through her whole body. In the time it took Angel to respond, my mind jumped from panic, to relief, and back to panic. I wished there was a way to lasso my words and shove them back where they came from. Once again, I'd let go of secrets that I'd promised to keep. I'd given them away, when I knew they weren't mine to give.

"Wow." Angel rubbed her temples. "I'll admit that's more than I expected."

Through the thick curtain of panic, a bit of relief crept back in. Maybe Angel could help. Maybe Angel would know what to do. I had struggled to do much right so far, but maybe this was my chance.

And so, when Angel asked, "Is there more you think you should tell me?" I told her. In a hushed and rushed voice, I told Angel Sweeney everything I knew. The whole big, sad mystery.

When I was done, I said, "So I think Cece does need help. But maybe not the kind of help she asked me for. Or that she wants to ask you for. And I don't know what to do."

Angel hadn't said anything while I spoke. She didn't stop me or ask any questions. She just nodded along. When I finished, she looked at me for a long time.

"You're helping her by being her friend."

Not this again. Not another grown-up telling me I was a good friend, when I was anything but that. I had failed Cece, and now I'd betrayed her trust too. I stared at my hands.

"Look at me, Lou."

I made my eyes look at her, but my head was too heavy to lift.

"Sometimes, as much as we want to change something for someone, we can't. All we can do is be there for them and help in small ways along their journey."

"How do I do that?" I asked.

"You tell her what you heard. Then you listen. You ask questions." Angel paused. "And in this case, you encourage Cece to talk to the person who might be able to help. Her father."

I considered her suggestions. The listening part was okay. But getting her to talk to her dad? I didn't think anyone could do that.

I stood.

"Thanks. For everything," I said. "And I'm sorry if we wasted your time. I never expected you to do a free reading anyway."

Angel smiled.

"You didn't waste my time. And I'm sorry your friend is going to be further disappointed."

"Me too."

I turned toward the door that led back to the living room.

"Lou?"

I spun around.

"I sense that you may feel out of control with the relationships in your life. You're in a time of learning and growth. It will all smooth itself out. Eventually."

I half smiled and turned back toward the door. Maybe that was my reading. My sign. I hoped what Angel said would become the truth.

31

I sat on one of the antique chairs in the living room petting Mercury and waiting for Cece. She stayed on the sun porch for what seemed like hours. Every time I checked the old grandfather clock in the corner of the room, though, I was surprised to see only a few minutes passed. Part of me hoped Angel would tell Cece about the phone call I'd overheard. I knew that made me a coward, but it didn't stop me from hoping.

When Cece stepped back into the living room, her face was blotchy and her eyes were shiny. I moved toward her, and a wall went up. Her eyes hardened, and she plastered on a smile.

"Okay! Thank you *so* much, Angel! Let's go, Lou."

As soon as we were outside and off Angel's porch, I turned to Cece again. Her face was glued into that forced smile.

"That was incredible! I knew that would be worth it.

She confirmed everything. My dad and grandmother are wrong. My mom is searching as hard as she can for me. And get this."

I stopped walking. Cece turned to face me.

"Angel said we were right to follow the signs to Kansas City. My mom is there. And if we go, there's still a chance we can fix everything. Do you believe that?"

The wall dropped a little. Cece's eyes softened and they pleaded with me. Even though I knew she was lying, I wanted nothing more than to hug her and tell her that together we could fix her family. But we couldn't. So I didn't. I nodded slowly. And because I didn't know what to say to make it okay, I didn't say anything.

~

We walked in silence until we reached the end of Angel's street. Cece turned right toward her apartment and downtown, and I turned left. My stomach was tied in a million knots. And my heart ached almost as badly as it had the day I said the terrible, horrible things.

My brain was caked in mud so thick, not a single coherent thought could poke through. I'd work out a plan once I got home. I'd figure out how to tell Cece the truth in the privacy of my room with the help of my notebook.

James's beat-up truck was in the driveway when I got home. I hoped I'd be able to slip by him without being asked too many questions.

I opened the door and Tripp flew out from behind the couch.

"Boo! Did I scare you?" He held his hands over his head

like claws. He was wearing a Batman mask, and Lady Rainbow's head poked out of his backpack.

"Terrified me." I fake-shivered and walked past him to my room.

"Guess what I learned today at school?" Tripp pattered after me down the hall.

"Hey honey girl! How was your day?" Mom called from the kitchen. She was at the kitchen table bouncing Orla on her knee. James stood in front of the refrigerator.

"Fine. Got a lot of homework." I opened the door to my room. Tripp followed me in.

"No time for even a proper hello?" James called after me.

"Sorry. Hi. I'll come out for dinner. Just want to start so I'm not up late."

Tripp bounced on my bed.

"You didn't guess," he said.

"Guess what?"

"What I learned at school."

I sighed.

"I don't know. I give up. What did you learn at school today, Tripp?"

"Pedo means 'fart' in Spanish!" He rolled back on my bed and laughed so hard his eyes closed.

"They taught you that at daycare? That's . . . something. Now can you go?"

Tripp rolled around on my bed making farting noises. I pulled him off and nudged him toward the door. He skipped away without a fight. After I shut the door, I sat on my bed with my notebook and pulled my knees into my chest.

A couple years ago, before Orla was born, I had been in the family room pretending to read a book while Mom and Nannie argued on the couch. Mom told Nannie that she was thinking of going back and trying college again, and Nannie listed all the reasons she didn't think it was a good idea: college was expensive, Mom had two kids, she was stressed enough as it was. Everything Nannie said, Mom had an answer for: she'd take out loans, there was plenty of family around to help, following her dreams would make her less stressed in the long run.

Eventually, Nannie threw up her hands and said, "You're chasing the wind, Jenny."

Mom had stormed off into the kitchen, and Nannie went home soon after. Not long after that, Mom told me she was pregnant with Orla. She never went back to school.

I thought about this conversation sometimes, but the part that I thought about now was what Nannie said about chasing the wind. That was exactly what Cece was doing. Chasing after something—someone—she was never going to catch. Believing in something that was never going to happen.

And I was letting her do it. I knew she was wrong. But I was too much of a coward to do anything about it. I was the worst friend in the world all over again.

I tried using my notebook to plan the conversation I needed to have with Cece. But only one thought made it out onto the paper.

Cece is chasing the wind. Cece is chasing the wind. Cece is chasing the wind.

32

FIFTH GRADE

The Holy Smokes Barbeque Festival was the unofficial start to summer at Our Lady of Perpetual Help. It was a blur of bounce houses, face painting, funnel cakes, and delicious barbeque. The whole parish came out. Francie and I went together every year.

We had a routine.

Face painting first, before the line got too long. Funnel cake and snow cones until we felt sick. Kickball in the empty field next to the barbeque tents.

And when the game ended, we got my notebook out of Mom's car. We snuck around under the twinkle lights spying on grown-ups and writing all the juicy stuff that would never make it into roundup published in the Mayfield Gazette *that week.*

Mrs. Brewer—too-tight shirt, laughing loudly at Mr. Murphy's jokes.

Clay Johnson and Jessica Martinez—fighting behind the bounce house. Jessica ripped keys from Clay's hand—stormed off.

Father Fred—sleeping in a lawn chair at Mr. Maguire's BBQ tent. Overheard Mr. Maguire say, "Looks like someone hit the communion wine a little too hard."

That's what we wrote at the end of fourth grade.

At Holy Smokes at the end of fifth grade, Francie and I met at the bounce house, like usual. We said we'd meet there at six. Francie showed up at six thirty. Her hair was straighter and blonder than ever, and there was something different about her eyes.

"You're late. There's already a line for face painting. Why do you look different?"

I couldn't keep the accusation out of my voice.

Francie ignored it. "Do you like my hair? Bernie did it for me with her straightening iron. Maybe she could do yours sometime." Francie cocked her head to the side and studied my hair.

I ran my hand over my thick, dark curls. Bernie was finishing seventh grade. She wore eyeliner, never stopped looking at her phone, and terrified me.

"Yeah, sure," I said, although there was no way I was letting Bernie near me with a hot iron. "Let's get going. I don't want to spend the whole time waiting in line. Father Fred got here fifteen minutes ago, and he already looked a little out of it. There's going to be plenty of action tonight. I can already tell."

"Are you sure?" Francie asked.

"Yeah, he's already over at the Maguire's tent again, and—"

"No, I meant about the face painting."

"Yes, there are already a bunch of kids over there. If we don't hurry—"

"No. I mean are you sure you want to get your face painted? We're going to be sixth graders, after all."

My face got hot. Francie might as well have kicked me in the stomach.

"I don't if you don't," I stammered. "There's tons of other stuff to do."

"Oh, okay, good." She sounded relieved. "Tommy asked me to meet him at his dad's barbeque tent, but let's get a snow cone first."

"We always get funnel cake first." I struggled to keep the whine out of my voice.

"A snow cone sounds better. It's hot out. Is everything okay?"

I didn't know how to tell her it wasn't. I didn't even know why it wasn't. I just nodded.

"Are you sure? We can get a funnel cake if you want," Francie said. She studied my face.

"No, you're right. A snow cone sounds great," I said, even though it didn't.

~

The night went on like that.

This is what I wrote in my notebook when I got home:

What I learned at the Holy Smokes BBQ:

1. Sixth grade is too old for face painting or bounce houses.

2. Francie talks to Tommy Maguire on the phone (on Bernie's phone? Her mom's phone? Did Francie get a phone?)

3. Cherry snow cones make you look like you're wearing lipstick—(do NOT order blueberry next time).

4. Francie thinks Tommy is hilarious. Nothing he said was funny.

That was the first time I understood what Nannie meant that day in the living room with Mom. It was the first time I realized that no matter how badly I wanted it, Francie might never be the old Francie again—the first time I understood what it was to chase the wind.

33

A good night's sleep did a world of good. I knew I needed to talk to Cece, and more importantly, that I *could* talk to her. We were going to her apartment again after school, to work on our essay. Cece wanted to plan our trip to Kansas City, too, but I hadn't asked Dad, and I figured after we talked she'd understand why. It would be far more painful to chase a mother who didn't want to be found than to face the truth. At least that's what I told myself. And I prayed Cece would see it the same way.

At her apartment, Cece went straight to the kitchen, as usual. There was a note on the counter.

Cee, I went for a walk. Needed the exercise, but I'll be back in an hour or so. Love you! –Dad

Cece read it, wordlessly shoved Dr Peppers into my hands and hightailed it down the hall. I tucked my leather-bound notebook under my arm so I wouldn't drop the drinks. Instead of opening her bedroom door, Cece opened her dad's.

I scurried after her.

"What are you doing?" I whispered, even though there was no one else there to hear me.

"This." Cece opened her dad's top dresser drawer and pulled out a wad of bills. "We're going to need this to get to the airport, right?"

She shoved the bills in her pocket, grabbed one of the Dr Peppers out of my hand, and walked across the hall to her bedroom.

"He never takes walks. It's another sign telling us we're on the right path." Cece plopped onto her bed and opened the soda can. Her eyes were so full of hope, it almost stopped me from saying what I knew I needed to say. Almost.

I set my notebook and the other Dr Pepper on Cece's desk. I took a deep breath, summoned every bit of courage inside me, and prayed one last time that this was the right thing.

"I-don't-think-we-should-go-to-Kansas-City." I forced the words out, like I was ripping off a Band-Aid.

"What? Why not?"

I closed my eyes. Then I told Cece what I should've told her a week ago.

"I overheard a conversation. A phone call. Between your parents. It sounded like your mom wanted space. And that she might be traveling somewhere. Alone."

Cece forced out a laugh that sounded more like a bark and shook her head. "That's ridiculous. You must've misheard."

"I didn't."

"Then you must've gotten it mixed up. Maybe whatever my dad said made it seem like that, but I'm sure you're wrong."

I had no idea what to say next. What would someone who was good at this kind of thing say? Someone like Francie.

"That's not all," I continued. "She was here. On Thursday. I saw her outside of school, checking on you or something."

Cece held the edge of her comforter and twisted it in her hands.

"That's impossible," she snapped.

"I heard your dad say something to her about it on the phone. He seemed pretty upset. You need to talk to him."

"I don't believe you. And of course he's upset. This whole situation is his fault. He could fix it if he wanted to."

"Maybe. Or maybe he can't. I just don't think going to Kansas City is a good idea. At least not until you talk to him."

"What about the clues? The signs? I thought you were on my side."

"I am on your side. But I think that maybe—maybe he's not lying to you."

"How can you say that? After everything?" The wall Cece built around herself at Angel's sprung back. Her eyes hardened.

"I don't know. I'm just thinking that maybe everything we've found, the clues, maybe they're actually pointing us toward what your dad has been saying."

"And what exactly do you think he's saying?" Her voice was as stormy as her eyes.

"It's just that—"

"That what? You don't believe me? You're on *my dad's* side now?"

"No. I'm just saying that maybe—"

"Maybe what, Lou? Go ahead. Say it."

I didn't let myself think.

"Maybe your mom's not looking for you."

The color drained from Cece's face, like she had the wind knocked out of her. She didn't speak for a solid minute. I held my breath, hoping, praying that she would understand. I didn't want to hurt her. The last thing I wanted was to lose her, too. But once again, no amount of hoping or praying could fix the mess I'd gotten into.

"Get out," Cece hissed.

"Cece—"

"No. I mean it. I want you to leave."

"But, I—"

"Call your mom, or walk or something. I don't care. I don't want you here."

Her voice regained its calm, but she still had the look of stunned betrayal. A look I knew well. It was the same look Francie had had after I said the terrible, horrible things.

"Okay. If that's what you want." I fought back tears as I gathered my things.

"It is." Cece stood by the door ready to usher me out.

My eyes blurred and my legs were Jell-O, but I made it out of the apartment and into the stairwell. I shoved the heavy door open, and it nearly hit Mr. Duncan as I hurried out to the lobby.

"Lou! Whoa. Where's the fire?" Mr. Duncan chuckled at his own joke. Then he saw my face. "Is everything okay? Where's Cece?"

"I'm fine. I just have to—I have to go." I shoved the words out around the lump in my throat.

"Lou?"

I didn't answer. I couldn't. I brushed by him and willed my feet to find the way home.

34

My head wanted to run straight home, but my heart wasn't ready to face Mom. Either she wouldn't notice anything was wrong, or she'd ask a million questions. Both options made me nauseous. Instead, I skulked around town like a stray cat, fighting tears and praying I wouldn't run into anyone I knew. I walked toward the south side of town—Francie's side. When I got to Casey's General Store, I pictured me and Francie sitting outside on the curb sharing a cherry Sprite and a pack of Starbursts. We used to treat ourselves every time we saved enough change. I turned around before my tears could win. I passed school and the church and then the library.

I wandered up one street and down another, feeling out of place on familiar streets. It was like being at Our Lady of Perpetual Help the day after I said the terrible, horrible things. Moms called their kids in for dinner. Bikes and balls were put away. Kitchen lights glowed. And the ache in my heart threatened to swallow me whole.

I forced myself to make a turn that would lead toward home, when it hit me like a knee to the stomach. My notebook. I dropped to the ground right where I was. I rummaged through my backpack. No notebook. I dumped the contents on the ground. No notebook. I opened the front pocket and the hidden pocket inside. No notebook.

I stuffed my math book and old assignments and stray pencils back in my bag. I closed my eyes. I pictured exactly where the notebook sat. On the edge of Cece's desk. *Thirty. Twenty-nine. Twenty-eight.*

I got down to zero before I moved. I had to go back. There was no other choice.

The things I'd written ran circles around my brain— *Good Things About Francie Hating Me, Reasons Why I Can't Help Cece,* and worst of all—*Reasons Why I Hate the New Francie.*

My heart raced. And my legs must've wanted to catch my heart, because they carried me faster than I knew they could run.

In minutes I was outside Able & Payne and Cece's apartment. I flew through the doors and up the stairs. Without giving myself time to think, I pounded on the door.

No answer. I pounded again.

This time I heard footsteps in the hall, slow and plodding. The door opened and Mr. Duncan stood shadowy and backlit in the dim light that streamed from the kitchen.

"Lou, hi."

"Hi. I, um, can I come in?"

When Mr. Duncan didn't move aside, I added, "I left a notebook here."

"You know, I don't think Cece's up for visitors right now."

"That's okay. I'll be quick."

"I think it's best if she brings it back to you at school tomorrow. Okay? But, hey, is your mom still downstairs? Do you need to call for a ride?"

"Um, yeah. She's downstairs," I lied.

The landing spun and the narrow stairwell closed in on me. I needed to get out of there. Without saying goodbye, I turned and raced down the stairs. I burst out of the building and onto the sidewalk. The sky glowed pink, but the evening air was heavy. No matter how deeply I sucked it in, I couldn't get enough to fill my lungs. I wanted to believe Cece would return the notebook, unopened, unread. But that wall around her, the hardness in her eyes. I knew better than anyone that anger—and fear—made people do things they wouldn't normally do. Terrible things. Horrible things. Things they would take back a million times over. If only it were possible to go backward.

~

By the time I reached my house, I had forced myself to believe that this would blow over. Cece was mad at her dad, and maybe now her mom, but not me. We'd both read *Harriet the Spy*, and she wouldn't want what happened to Harriet to happen to me. When Harriet's friends found her notebook, they read everything, and then they hated her because of it. Cece had a notebook of her own. She knew how awful that would be.

Mom and James were on the couch when I walked in.

"I cannot sit through something that requires that much thinking right now," Mom said as I eased the door open. I hoped I could slide past them to my room. That they'd be too busy to bother asking me questions. Wrong.

"Hey, sweetheart! I put the leftovers from dinner in the fridge for you. Did you girls get a lot done on your essay? You were there longer than I thought you'd be." Then Mom must've noticed something in my face, because her smile faded, and her forehead wrinkled the way it does when she's worried.

"What's wrong? Did something happen?"

"Feeling okay, kiddo?" James asked. He sounded serious, too.

"I'm fine. And I don't want to talk about it." My voice was sharper than I meant it to be. "If that's okay, I mean."

"Honey girl, are you sure? Why don't you sit with us? It might help to talk it out," Mom said.

I knew it wouldn't.

"I'm tired." I'd made it across the living room and was standing in the doorway that led to the hallway.

Mom stood. James pulled her gently back onto the couch.

"Why don't we give her space tonight, Jenny. Maybe she'll feel up to talking in the morning."

I gave James a grateful half-smile. If his hand weren't on Mom's knee, gently holding her in place, I'm pretty sure she would've come after me. I was glad she didn't.

35

The next morning, I stayed in bed with the covers pulled over my head for as long as I could. By the way the sun beat in through my window, I knew that if I didn't come out soon, Mom would come in. Then I'd really be trapped.

Mom appeared in the hallway as soon as I opened my bedroom door. She'd been waiting for me. I smelled cinnamon and bacon coming from the kitchen. Usually that smell would've had me bouncing out of bed. Now it made the knot in my stomach tighten.

"Good morning, sleepyhead." Mom tousled my hair. I ducked away and followed my nose to the kitchen. Maybe if I acted like nothing had happened, she would, too.

"What's for breakfast?" I tried my best to sound cheerful. I hoped my voice didn't come out as fake as it felt.

James flipped French toast on an electric skillet as bacon sizzled in a frying pan behind him. Orla was in her high chair and Tripp stood in front of her playing peekaboo. Every time he moved his hands away from his eyes, she squealed. I wanted to stay here forever. I would eat James's cooking, play with my brother and sister, and pretend Cece and Francie and the entire sixth grade didn't exist.

"This is for these crazies," James said, gesturing toward Tripp and Orla. "I think your mama has something special planned for the two of you."

As if on cue, Mom came up behind me.

"I thought we could use a little Mom/Lou time. What if we head downtown for some donuts at Nettie's? It finally feels like fall around here, and I've been craving one of her apple fritters."

"What about school? It's time to leave. And don't you have to be at work?"

"I called us both in already. Told Sister Margaret and my boss that we needed some extra time this morning. James is going to take care of these two."

I knew Mom wanted to talk, but the thought of telling her how badly I'd hurt Francie and messed everything up with Cece made my stomach roll. I wanted to tell Mom that I would rather stay here and eat James's French toast.

But I figured I'd ruined enough with my words lately.

"Sure, Mom."

~

By the time we got downtown, it was after nine o'clock.

Mom was right. Fall had settled on Mayfield overnight. The air was crisp, and for the first time, I noticed the bright red and orange leaves of the oak trees that lined Market Street. It's weird how that happens. It's like you wake up one morning and they're different. But they must have been slowly changing all along.

Mom found a parking spot outside of Nettie's Apron. It felt like fall inside the bakery, too. The smell of apple, pumpkin, and hot chocolate. We got our food, and nestled into a booth by the windows that looked out onto the street. Mom wasted no time.

"Lou, I'm sorry." She rubbed the bridge of her nose and then wrapped her hands around her coffee mug.

"It's okay." Maybe this would be the end of it. Not so bad.

"No, it's not. You've been going through something, and I've been so wrapped up in *me* that I haven't given you the time you deserve."

"Mom, really, it's okay."

"What's going on with you and Francie? And I mean what's *really* going on?"

Maybe it was the way she looked at me like I was a little kid again. Maybe it was the way she reached across the table and grabbed my hand. Maybe it was that everything had been bubbling inside me for so long that it was bound to spill over eventually. I don't know.

What I do know is that I burst into wet, hot, embarrassing tears right there at the table. I couldn't talk, and I had to wipe snot away with the back of my hand.

"Oh honey. I'm so, so sorry. It's going to be okay. I promise."

"What if it's not?" I managed to say through shuddery sobs. "I ruined everything."

"I'm sure that's not true."

Mom moved to my side of the booth. She wrapped her arm around me and stroked my hair. I hoped her back blocked anyone inside Nettie's from seeing what a baby I was.

"I—" I struggled to make my mouth say the words. "I really, really hurt them."

"Who? Francie?"

"Francie and Cece. And there's no way for me to fix it. They hate me, and I deserve it. It's just ... It's just ..."

"That you're hurt, too?" Mom finished for me.

I nodded and nestled further into her.

We sat there like that for a long time. She stroked my hair and let me cry, until I took a shaky breath and sat up. Like I had at Angel's, I let the whole, awful, messy truth out.

When I finished, Mom was quiet for a long time. Then she looked me in the eye.

"You know, Lou, if there's one thing that's certain, it's that people make mistakes. No one is perfect, and sometimes we mess up the most in the relationships that matter the most."

I didn't say anything. Mom took a long sip of her coffee, and then she continued.

"Sometimes we mix up the way we feel about ourselves or our own struggles with anger toward other people. I know I do. I've said plenty of things I regret. To Nannie. To James. To you."

She looked at me sideways over her mug.

"And you know something else?"

I shook my head.

"Messing up doesn't make someone a bad person. Look at me. I've messed up so many times, I've lost count. But I'm not a bad person. At least I don't think I am, do you?"

I shook my head. A smile tugged at the corner of my mouth.

"And you're not a bad person either. And neither is Francie. Or Cece. You're all just humans who are hurt. You hear me?"

I nodded.

"But . . . what you decide to do next matters, too."

We ate the rest of our apple fritters as I let Mom's words roll around inside me. I thought they might have unraveled the knot in my stomach the tiniest bit. When we were getting ready to clear the table, Mom spoke again.

"Honey girl, I think you know what you need to do." She brushed a curl that had fallen in front of my eye behind my ear. "Start with talking. I'm not saying that will fix everything. Sometimes things change between people, and that's just the way it is. But you won't feel better until Francie and Cece know how truly sorry you are for hurting them."

I nodded. I knew Mom was right. I just didn't know how to make something that was supposed to be simple not feel like the hardest thing in the world.

36

When I got to school, chatter and laughter drifted into the hallway from Mrs. Jackson's classroom. The class must have been taking the mid-morning Brain Break. In between subjects, Mrs. Jackson set a timer for ten minutes and let us stretch, talk, and move around the room to "rest our brains." This was perfect. I could slip in, hand Mrs. Jackson my tardy slip, and take my seat unnoticed.

Wrong.

A hush fell over the classroom as soon as I walked through the door. All eyes were on me the way they were the day after I said the terrible, horrible things. I tried to escape by going into the coatroom, where I found Madison Brewer digging in her backpack. She looked me up and down like she was deciding if she should say what she wanted to say. It was Madison, so of course she decided to say it.

"You messed things up with Cece, too, huh?"

I stared at her. I made my face as blank as possible.

"I shouldn't tell you this, but you're going to find out anyway." Madison glanced at the door that led into the classroom to make sure no one was coming. "It wasn't smart of you to leave your notebook sitting around like that. Everyone's *really* mad."

The coatroom spun. I reached for the wall to keep from falling over.

Madison gave me a pained smile.

"Don't worry, Lou. I'm sure they'll move on to something else. Eventually."

She turned on her heel and flounced out.

Thirty. Twenty-nine. Twenty-eight. My legs were heavy and stuck to that spot like they'd been cemented to the ground. With each number, I reminded myself to breathe.

I could see the timer on the board had reached its final countdown. Mrs. Jackson would call the class back together in less than a minute. I shrunk into myself and slinked to my seat, willing Mrs. Jackson to silence the class early. She stood in the doorway holding a stack of papers and talking to Sister Margaret, seemingly oblivious to the noise behind her. I laid my head on my arm and instinctively reached for my notebook. There was nothing to reach for.

But then I saw it. The brown leather edge of my notebook. It sat in Braden's lap.

"Looks like Lou doesn't think your jokes are funny, Tommy." Braden chuckled and elbowed Tommy in the ribs.

"What? Impossible. I'm hilarious. Let me see that." Tommy grabbed my notebook out of Braden's lap. He slid it under his own desk and flipped through the pages.

"*Reasons Why I Hate the New Francie*," Tommy read aloud. "Hey Francie, this one's about you."

Francie spun around. I fought the urge to run out of the room.

Before he could read from the list, the timer went off. Sister Margaret bustled away, and Mrs. Jackson closed the door, seemingly unaware that my entire life had shattered to pieces right there in her classroom.

I knew Cece was two rows behind me, but I didn't dare turn around. Her betrayal stung.

As the class settled back into their seats, I prayed vocabulary or journals were next, anything that required silence and no movement.

"Boys and girls, our Christ Is Alive! essays are due on Monday. The assembly and awards presentation will be the following week. This is the last time we'll work on the essays during class," Mrs. Jackson said.

I kept the corner of my eye trained on my notebook. It sat on the corner of Tommy's desk. I plotted how I could walk by and snatch it back without creating a scene. I could tell Mrs. Jackson, but what if she confiscated it? Or asked questions I didn't want to answer?

"Mrs. Jackson, Lou and I finished our essay last night," Cece called out. This was news to me. "Do you think it would be alright if we worked on something else during this time? *Separately?*"

Francie leaned forward in her seat and shot her hand into the air.

"Cece can sit with us," she said without Mrs. Jackson's permission to speak. "Just for today. We're almost done, too."

"That'll be fine, Francie," Mrs. Jackson said absently. She was at her desk fiddling with her computer, trying to get the essay rubric to project on the board.

It took everything in me not to burst into tears. The classroom closed in. I needed my notebook.

As soon as Mrs. Jackson gave us permission to move, I beelined straight toward Tommy. He saw me coming and slid the notebook inside his desk. Then he scooched forward until his stomach was pressed against the desk pocket. Short of knocking him to the ground and wrestling him for it, there was no way I was getting it back.

I spun around and nearly walked right into Cece. We locked eyes for a second.

"They deserved to know what you think about them." Then she stared at the ground. "To know that you write one thing while you say another."

Cece's words nearly bowled me over. I turned away from her and raced out of the room without even asking Mrs. Jackson for the bathroom pass.

Once the stall door was closed behind me, I slid onto the floor. I pulled my knees to my chest and let my tears take over. I needed to be anywhere but here. Once I stopped the shuddery, I've-been-crying-my-eyes-out breathing, I went down the hall to the nurse's office. I told her I'd thrown up in the girls' bathroom. She gave me a cold pack for my head and let me lie on a cot with the curtain pulled around me while I waited for Mom to come get me. I counted backward until I dozed off. This time, I started at one hundred.

37

THE FOURTH DAY OF SIXTH GRADE

In the time between coming home from Kansas City and the start of sixth grade, I had slept over at Francie's house as many nights as I slept at my own house. It had been like Francie and I were constantly playing a game of tug-of-war. I dug my heels in trying my best to pull her back in the direction we'd come from. But she was walking effortlessly with her end of the rope in the opposite direction.

Once school started, our weekday sleepovers were put on hold, but the first Saturday of sixth grade, I wasted no time. As soon as I finished lunch, I packed my bag and waited by the door until Mom was ready to take me to Francie's.

When I arrived, Francie's younger sister, Tess, was practicing piano in the front room. She banged away on the keyboard, making as much noise as possible. Mrs. Fitzpatrick lay on the couch in her bathrobe watching old game show reruns, like she couldn't hear Tess's racket. It was two o'clock in the afternoon.

I followed the sound of Francie's voice to her bedroom.

"It's not your phone anymore!" Francie screeched as Bernie pulled a cell phone out of Francie's hands and held it over her head. "We share it!"

Bernie had gotten a phone when she started sixth grade, and at the beginning of summer, their parents had informed her that now that Francie was starting sixth grade, it was a shared phone. Fifty-fifty.

"Give it to me, or I'm literally *going to get Mom." Francie jumped in the air and tried grabbing the phone from Bernie. Francie used the word* literally *excessively lately, even when it didn't fit. Bernie glanced in the direction of the living room where their mother lay on the couch.*

"Okay, fine. But if you text anything weird to my friends, I'll literally *dye your hair while you're sleeping." Bernie gave Francie a look so mean it made the hair on my arms stand straight. Francie grabbed the phone and flopped onto her bed.*

We spent the next several hours lying on our backs on Francie's bed looking up things like what colors were most flattering to our complexions and how to get your crush to text you back.

"Do you think I'm pretty?" Francie asked suddenly, propping herself up on her elbow. "As pretty as Bernie?"

"Of course," I said, and I did.

"Do you think Tommy thinks so? I think he might want to ask me out." Francie lay back down and scrolled through her contacts.

"Out to where?" I dug my heels in and pulled the rope back as hard as I could.

"Out to nowhere. To be his girlfriend. Braden told me he's been thinking it for a while now."

I stared at the ceiling, fighting the urge to grab the phone out of her hands.

"Don't you think sixth grade is kind of young for a boyfriend? I mean, we have our whole lives for that." I sounded like someone's mother. And not even my own mother, because she wouldn't be upset if she heard Francie wanted a boyfriend.

"Maybe if Tommy asks me out, then Braden will ask you out. That would be literally perfect." She pulled up Tommy's name and typed a message.

"I thought he liked Madison?" I knew we'd spend the rest of the night texting stupid Tommy Maguire, but I would put my foot down at Braden Kelly.

"If he does, that's dumb, and I'm sure I could get him to change his mind. You're prettier than her and obviously way smarter."

I continued staring at the ceiling.

Francie typed away without telling me what she wrote. Every now and then I glanced over, but it was hard to read the screen over her shoulder, and I didn't care that much anyway.

"Oh my God. This is it!" She popped into a sitting position. "They want to hang out later tonight. They say we should sneak out and meet them." She squealed.

"Who's they?"

"Tommy and Braden. They're at Braden's house."

"Francie, this is not a great idea. What if we get caught?"

"We won't. And even if we do, my mom won't say anything. It's fine."

~

I spent the rest of the evening praying Francie would change her mind. But as soon as her parents and Tess were asleep, and Bernie was watching a movie in the basement, Francie pulled the phone out and texted Tommy.

They made a plan to meet at the playground between her house and Braden's. Sweat pooled under my arms as we crept into the front hallway. The sound of Francie turning the lock and opening the door echoed throughout the house, but Francie acted like it was the middle of the day. I followed her lead.

When we got to the playground, Tommy and Braden were swinging on the old swing set. I couldn't remember the last time I'd swung as high as they were going.

"Francie, you want a turn?" Tommy said. "Braden, give her your swing."

Francie squeezed my hand and then smoothed her hair. "Do I look okay?"

Before I answered she skipped over to the swing set. Braden jumped out of his swing, Tommy slowed his, and Francie hopped on where Braden had been.

I wasn't sure what I was supposed to do, so I sat on one of the wood logs that lined the playground. Despite willing him not to, Braden sat next to me. Tommy and Francie swung slowly, side by side.

I'd known Braden since I was five years old, but I don't think I'd ever talked to him outside of school.

"So, what'd you think of that science experiment yesterday?" We'd made batteries out of vegetables.

"Uh. That it was lame."

Dumb me should've stopped there.

"I thought the apple would generate the most power. But the potato? Who knew?" I forced out a laugh that was more of a cross between choking and grunting.

"You are so weird." Braden scooted away from me on the log.

We sat in uncomfortable silence as Tommy and Francie got off their swings. Tommy leaned in close like he was telling her a secret. I could see her grin through the dim glow coming from the streetlight. Then he inched closer, pecked her lips, shoved his hands in his pockets, and walked away from the playground.

"Braden, let's go," he yelled.

I stood, reeling. It was like I'd fallen face-first into the mud as Francie walked away with the rope.

38

I managed to make it home from the nurse's office before I burst into tears again. I told Mom what happened, and then, for the second time that day, I let Mom stroke my hair, rub my back, and tell me that everything would be okay. I stayed curled on the couch for the rest of the afternoon. Even Tripp didn't bother me.

Mom let me stay home from school the next day, which has never happened in the history of ever. Even when I'm actually sick, she's ready to push me back out the door as soon as I'm up and moving around.

I stayed snuggled on my spot on the couch under a thick layer of blankets. Mom took off work to sit with me, and Nannie came over, too. They watched soap operas and got me all my favorite snacks. Nannie only tried making me talk three times, which for her is some kind of record.

Mom agreed to let me stay home for the weekend, instead of going to Kansas City, which was another first.

Her only requirement was that I had to call Dad myself to make sure it was okay.

The phone rang three times before he answered.

"Hello?"

"Hi, Dad. It's me, Lou."

"Honey, hi. What's going on?"

"If it's okay with you—do you think it would be okay if I came to see you a different weekend? There's some stuff going on here and—"

"What's going on? Is everything okay?"

I took a deep breath. It was a question I'd expected but didn't know how to answer.

"Not really. But if it's okay, can I tell you about it when we're together?"

My answer surprised even me. Mostly because I meant it. I wanted to tell him.

"Of course. I'm sure your mom's got it under control, huh?"

"Yeah. She does. But if you're not working I could come in a couple weeks?"

"I'm off for three weeks, so that's great with me. But it's Halloween. You sure you want to spend that here?"

Halloween was a big deal in Mayfield—a parade on Market Street, costume contests, a festival at the municipal park, and hours of trick-or-treating. Missing it sounded absolutely perfect. And I told him so.

I stayed in my spot all day Saturday, too. I pretended that none of it had ever happened. I pretended that I'd be on that couch, safe and snuggled forever.

Then Mom sent me on an errand.

"Honey girl, do you think you're up for doing me a favor?" Mom sat next to me on the couch, Tripp cuddled up on my other side. We were watching *Frozen* for the second time that day.

"I don't know, Mom. We're getting to the best part."

Mom gave me a look.

"You can watch it again when you get back. It would do you a world of good to get out and stretch your legs. After all, it's back to school on Monday."

That's what I should've expected, but I was startled that she planned to push me back out into the wild so soon.

"What's the favor?" This time I gave *her* a look.

"I have some books on reserve at the library. Can you walk there and get them? You could pick out something for yourself, too, while you're there."

The tone of Mom's voice told me she'd decided. I wasn't getting out of this.

"Okay, fine." I stood, and Tripp pulled my portion of the blanket around himself. His thumb was in his mouth, and his eyes glassed over as he stared at the screen. He wasn't going to miss me.

As I made my way to the library, I wondered about my notebook. Who had it now? Had they read everything? I didn't want to know. I wanted the whole mess to be over. I wanted to rewind time. I wanted to go back to when Tommy and Braden didn't matter. When Francie's secrets were safe. When I'd never been asked to solve problems that were too big to fix.

~

I picked up Mom's books, and then I took a left out of the library instead of a right. Going right would've taken me back to Fourth Street and home. Going left took me toward the south side of town. Francie's side.

My feet carried me there without my mind telling them to. I passed the markers that signaled I was getting closer—Our Lady of Perpetual Help, the three-story brick house where the nuns lived, Casey's General Store. I told myself I was just doing what Mom suggested. I was stretching my legs.

By the time I got to the playground, the one between Francie's house and Braden's house, the playground where everything fell apart, I stopped pretending. I knew what I was going to do.

I sat on the swing. And I waited. I waited until the sun turned a pumpkin-y orange and sunk behind the trees. I waited until the wind that kissed my cheek got a chill. I waited until I knew it had to be time.

I wanted to stop myself, but I couldn't figure out how. So instead, I let my feet pull me forward. I crept behind the houses that lined Francie's street and I made my way through the dusky pink light to Francie's backyard. Then I crawled through the hedges that lined the side of her house. I held my breath and prayed.

One by one, the girls from my class hopped out of their parents' cars carrying overnight bags. They headed inside to Francie's birthday sleepover.

I knew the car I was looking for was coming as soon as

it turned onto Francie's street. It was the small white car Cece's dad drove, much quieter than the trucks and minivans the other girls arrived in.

Cece's messy red ponytail popped out of the passenger side. She carried a duffel I'd never seen before and a sleeping bag.

She didn't wave as the white car backed out and pulled away.

I crawled forward a few feet, making sure I was still shielded by the hedge. Now I had eyes on the front door.

Cece rang the bell. Within seconds, Francie flung the door open, the light from inside hugging the space around her.

"Cece! I'm so happy you could come." Francie grabbed Cece and pulled her into the light.

As Francie released Cece from her embrace, she kept talking.

"We are going to have so much fun. We just ordered pizza and my dad said we can watch anything we want on Netflix."

She shut the front door behind them.

A thorn from the hedge dug into my arm and a tiny trail of blood ran from my elbow to my wrist. I stared at it, unable to wipe it away. I don't know how long I sat there, but the sun disappeared, and the sky went dark before I trusted my legs to stand and carry me home.

39

That night, sleep came in fits and spurts. I fell in and out of dreams that I could only remember in pieces.

I was finally pulled away from it by the bright morning light streaming through my window and my family clattering around in the living room. I looked at my alarm clock. 10:15. I never slept this late. Mom never *let* me sleep this late.

"Lady Rainbow will save the world from man-eating dragons!" Tripp yelled. His feet pattered around the house.

"You and Lady Rainbow can save the world at church. Quietly. Time to go," I heard Mom say. I pictured her grabbing jackets and frantically shoving extra snacks into Orla's diaper bag.

Mom never let me skip Mass, but considering I was still in my pajamas and buried under a pile of blankets, I guessed she'd decided to make an exception this week.

"Ugh. Orla needs new shoes *again*. James, can you get her feet into these? I'm going to check on Lou."

Orla shrieked and I knew James must've tickled her or made a funny face to get her to sit while he wrestled her chubby feet into church shoes. Mom's footsteps moved closer, and then she knocked softly on my door.

"Honey girl, are you up?"

I mumbled, "Yes," and then covered my head with my pillow. She opened the door.

"We're headed to Mass, but I figured you could use more rest."

"Thanks," I said from underneath my pillow.

When Mom didn't turn to go, I moved the pillow and peeked out.

"You sure you're okay?"

"I'm fine." And to prove it, I sat up. "But thanks for letting me stay home."

Before Mom could answer, her phone buzzed in her purse. She fumbled around inside her bag, and when the buzzing was about to stop, she pulled the phone out and answered it.

"This is Jenny."

It must've been a number she didn't recognize. That's how Mom always answers when she doesn't know the number.

"No. She wasn't at Francie's last night."

Long pause.

"Jenny," James called. "The kids are in the car. If we don't go now, we'll be late."

"You know what, she's right here. Would you like to talk to her?" Mom said into the phone. Then she held the phone out to me.

"It's Aaron Duncan," she whispered. "Call me on James's phone if you need me."

Then she called out to James, "I'm coming. You have your phone, don't you?"

My heart was in my throat. What was going on? Why would Mr. Duncan want to talk to me? And why would Mom leave me alone for this conversation?

I waited until the front door slammed shut behind Mom.

"H-h-ello?" I stammered.

"Lou! Hi! Aaron Duncan here. I was calling to see if you'd seen Cece this morning. Your mom said you hadn't, but I thought it'd be worth a shot to see if you know who she might be with."

"I haven't seen her, and I'm not sure. I didn't go to Francie's party." I let out my breath. It was a mix-up. This wasn't about the notebook. I wasn't in trouble.

"I see. Do you know who she might've gone home with? I went to pick her up, and Francie said she got a ride home. I didn't even think to ask with who, because I assumed it had to be you. You're the only friend of hers I've met. I guess I should never assume. Anyway, I'm rambling now, but if you don't know who it might be, I'll call the Fitzpatricks."

Francie said she got a ride home? I was as confused as Mr. Duncan. I didn't have the first clue as to who Cece would ask for a ride. He was right—until two days ago, the only person she talked to was me.

"I'm not sure. Sorry. Do you need Francie's home number?"

"No. I've got the school directory right here, but thanks, and sorry I bothered you."

After I hung up, I stared at the phone. I was relieved that Mr. Duncan's call was simple—that it had nothing to do with my notebook or Cece's mother or my failure as a friend. But something clawed at the corners of my mind. I wouldn't let my brain explore it, and when I tried shaking it, I couldn't, so I went back to my bed and buried myself under the covers instead.

~

When I couldn't fall asleep, I went to the kitchen to find a snack. I wasn't hungry, but my hollow stomach told me to feed it.

I poured a bowl of Cap'n Crunch. Mom's phone buzzed from where I'd left it in the living room. I almost ignored it—it was *her* phone—but curiosity got the best of me.

A number with no name attached lit the screen. It was the same number as before. Mr. Duncan.

"Hello?"

"Lou! Hi! Aaron Duncan again. Hey, I talked to Francie, she said her parents weren't home, and she didn't remember who took Cece home. Then she got flustered and said she had to go."

My brain buzzed, like tiny pieces of the puzzle were clicking together up there, one by one.

"I hate to bother you again, but I'm getting kind of worried. I'm not familiar with the kids in the class yet, so I was hoping you could help me out," Mr. Duncan continued.

The party was big, but not *that* big. Of course Francie would know who Cece had left with.

"Sure. I could give you some names to try." I slid onto the couch.

I rattled off the names of the girls I'd seen at the party, though I knew none of them would know where to find Cece. I stared at the dark TV screen, counting names on my fingers as I went. The time on the cable box glowed blue above the screen. The time blinked and then changed. And above it the date. October 18.

I knew. I knew exactly where Cece was. The final puzzle piece clicked into place. And I knew who'd helped her get there.

40

THE TENTH DAY OF SIXTH GRADE

In the days since Tommy had asked Francie to be his girl-friend and kissed her by the swing, she'd moved out of the space between Old Francie and New Francie. She was New Francie one hundred percent of the time.

I floated along trying to figure out what that meant for me.

Francie still chose me. I sat next to her at lunch. We went to her house after school. We had plans to spend the night at my house that Saturday.

But I felt Madison and Annabelle creeping in. Francie was curious about Madison's nail polish color and where Annabelle bought her new shoes. She had suggested I ask Mom if they could spend the night on Saturday, too.

I tried keeping my head above water, but most of the time I was gasping for air.

That Friday afternoon in August, we rode the bus to her house, like usual.

"Let's walk over to the park. The boys are practicing until

four thirty," Francie said as soon as we hopped off the bus onto her driveway.

"Mrs. Jackson assigned a lot of homework. I kind of want to get started so I'm not thinking about it all weekend."

We'd gone to football practice on Monday. And Wednesday.

Francie jutted out her lower lip and folded her hands like she was praying. "C'mon, Lou. Please? For me?"

"Okay, fine. I guess there's time later. Let's go."

Francie grinned.

We didn't even go inside to drop our backpacks. Or ask permission.

I'd barely seen Mrs. Fitzpatrick since school started. Every time I was at Francie's house, she was either in her bedroom or at Our Lady of Perpetual Help in the adoration chapel.

As we walked back toward downtown, Francie talked about the rest of the weekend.

"Did you ask your mom about Madison and Annabelle yet?"

"Not yet." I wasn't planning to, either.

"It will be so much fun. And I'm sure your mom will say yes. She's cool like that."

"Yeah, maybe."

"You could call her right now. I have my phone."

Francie pulled the phone she shared with Bernie out of the side pocket of her backpack.

"Now's not a good time," I said. "She's been really distracted lately."

"It's no big deal. She won't care if you call her."

She dangled the phone in front of me.

"Francie, I'm serious. I don't think I should call right now. She's at work."

"Okay, fine. Promise you'll ask when you get home?"

I nodded but anger rose through me like steam in a pot that's about to boil over.

When we got to the municipal park, Francie found us a seat on the bleachers closest to the field. She started clapping and yelling even though they were doing drills. I stuffed my frustration down and followed her lead. When the boys ran in lines around orange cones over and over, Francie got bored. She took her phone out.

We sat on the bleachers, and she mindlessly scrolled. She stopped scrolling and turned toward me.

"Lou! I have the best idea. Tommy gave me Braden's number. We should text him."

I froze. "How can we text him if he's practicing?"

"Silly, Braden doesn't play football."

That was news to me. To be honest, I couldn't tell who any of them were through their pads and helmets. I guess Francie didn't have the same problem.

"Okay. I sent it."

"Sent what?" The panic rose in my voice, and the anger I'd stuffed down crept back.

"Nothing, yet. I asked what he's doing."

"Seriously, Francie. Don't do this. I told you I don't like Braden."

"Too late. I asked him if he likes you." Francie smiled happily at the screen. "Look! He's typing."

I stopped protesting and watched over her shoulder. A

white speech bubble popped onto the screen. Francie moved to cover it, but I read what it said.

Gross. NO. Lou is SO weird. Not sure y ur friends with her.

I grabbed the phone out of Francie's hand.

"Lou. Don't get upset. I'm really sorry. He's just being Braden."

I held the phone out of her reach. Another bubble followed the first.

Not cute AT ALL. Total dog status.

"Did he say something else?" *Francie's eyes were wide, and she chewed on her bottom lip.* "I shouldn't have texted him. Seriously, ignore him. I don't know what I was thinking."

I let the phone fall from my hand.

Francie stood and looked to where the phone rolled under the bleachers into the dirt. She stepped toward me. "Lou..."

"I told you not to!" *I stood, too. I was yelling.*

"Don't get upset. I'm really sorry, but it's Braden. Everyone knows how he can be."

Then the anger spilled out and over everything.

"I can't believe you did that! I told you not to!" *My voice rose. I knew the boys on the sidelines could hear me. But I couldn't think past the static in my brain.*

"Lou. Stop. Everyone's staring at you," *Francie whispered.*

My anger was blistering. And the crazy thing is I wasn't even mad at Francie. I was mad that Braden had the power to hurt me like that. I didn't like him, but all that mattered was that he didn't like me. Like what I thought was less important. And that what he thought of me could make me less to Francie, too.

"Maybe I'm weird, but at least I know how to read. At least I didn't get all the way to sixth grade reading books for second graders."

The terrible, horrible things I couldn't unsay. Only, I wished I'd stopped there. My anger was so hot, it turned cold. And it spread and spread.

"Maybe if your mom cared about you a little more, maybe if she wasn't so busy praying and sleeping all the time, she'd know you barely made it out of fifth grade."

Just like that, time stopped. And my terrible, horrible, ugly words hung in the open air of Mayfield Municipal Park.

Francie turned toward the practice field. Half the team stood still. They stared right at us. When she turned back to me, her face shattered.

Now my words belonged to everyone who was there that day. And there was nothing I would ever be able to do to change that.

"I hate you," she hissed. Fat tears rolled down her cheeks. Then she jumped down from the bleachers and took off running.

41

I stared at Mom's phone for a long time after Mr. Duncan hung up. Francie's number scrolled through my mind like the time and temperature on the sign outside Mayfield Bank and Trust. Even though Francie had only had the phone since August and it was only half hers, I had the number memorized. I'd called it about a billion times. Half the times I called, I'd just left her house, but there was always more to say. Until there wasn't.

I typed the number, lost my nerve and cleared it, typed it again, lost my nerve again. I went to my room and grabbed a spiral notebook out of my backpack.

Where is Cece?

1. Did she try to get to Kansas City? If so, how?

2. What does Francie know?

3. Is Cece in danger?

I shivered.

Then I swallowed my fear and dialed the number, tapping the green call icon.

It rang three times before Francie answered.

"Hello?"

"Hi. It's me. It's Lou." My chest tightened.

"I know."

Silence hung between us. Words failed me, and I wished I'd thought to write what I wanted to say. A bulleted list, at least.

"I'm calling about Cece," I said finally.

"She's not here, and I've got to go." Francie sighed. I pictured her sitting on her bed cross-legged with her pillow in her lap. That's how she always sat when she talked on the phone. Maybe she was staring at the ceiling where we'd stuck glow-in-the-dark stars when we were in fourth grade. I loved those stars, but the last time I was there, Francie told me she wanted to take them down. I hoped she hadn't.

"Wait. Don't hang up," I pleaded.

No response.

"Do you know where she is?"

Tess practiced the piano in the background. Like always, it was closer to hammering than music. I don't know why, but *that* was what made me want to cry.

"Francie, please. I don't know what Cece told you, but the story is complicated. I'm worried about her."

If it weren't for Tess's piano playing, I would've thought she was gone.

"I'm worried, too," Francie whispered. "Meet me at the school playground in fifteen minutes? Under the slide?"

Then before I could answer, Francie hung up.

~

Mom, James, and the kids were still at church when I left, so I wrote a hasty note and left it for them on the kitchen counter.

Went to meet Francie. I'll explain everything later. Love, Lou

I got to school in record time, but Francie beat me. Her back was pressed against the slide's ladder and her ponytail hung over one of the rungs. A backpack was on the ground next to her. She turned around when she heard me coming.

"Took you long enough, geez."

Such a Francie thing to say.

"Where did Cece go?" I asked.

"What's going on with Cece?" Francie said at the exact same time.

We both fell silent and half smiled. It was so familiar, it hurt.

"You go first." I waved Francie on.

Francie stared at the underside of the slide. I went and sat beneath it so she had to look at me.

"I think Cece's in trouble. And I think it's my fault." Francie fiddled with the sleeves of her jacket and then crossed her arms. "And I know you're just going to think I was being stupid again, but—"

My heart jumped into my throat. "I've never thought anything you've ever done was stupid," I whispered.

Francie pretended she didn't hear me. "Cece ran away. She's in Kansas City. And I'm the one who helped her get there."

I wanted to ask, *What are we going to do?* But I let Francie finish talking.

"It started last night—at the sleepover. Me and Cece stayed up later than everyone else. And we were talking. My mom never came out of her room during the whole party, not even to say hi to my friends. And I was mad about it. So, I told Cece. I'd heard some stuff about her mom, so I thought she might understand. And then she told me what happened with her family. And how her mom is trying to find her. And she was so sad, you know?"

I pictured Cece unpacking her shoebox full of clues. I pictured her face when I told her I didn't think her mom was looking for her.

"And she told me that she knew her mom was in Kansas City and if she had a way to get there, everything would be okay. And so, I kind of told her how to do it. And gave her money. And helped her buy the ticket."

Francie's eyes dropped to her lap. She picked at her nails.

"I know it was dumb, but I also know what it's like to have a messed-up family, and I thought maybe this was my chance to help someone else."

I pictured Mrs. Fitzpatrick. I pictured her on the couch in her bathrobe in the middle of the day. I pictured her sitting at Francie's kitchen table with her eyes closed, rosary beads in hand, mouthing the words to the Hail Mary. And then there was what I'd said about her that day at the park.

"What did you tell her to do? And where'd you get the money?"

"I told her how to take the train to Kansas City. I remembered when you did it to go see your dad. And I remembered that time you said your mom was running late for something and couldn't go in with you to drop you off. How they had your release form saved in their system and they let you through with a note."

I remembered that trip. I'd been so nervous that they'd turn me away, but Mom had assured me it would be fine. And it was. I nodded.

"My mom keeps her purse on a hook in the kitchen. Her wallet is in there." Francie shrugged. "So, we went in there, and easy peasy. Credit card.

"We ordered tickets on my dad's laptop. In your name. I figured if they checked the system, that release would be in there." Francie's cheeks were pink and she had that look she gets when she doesn't want me to be mad at her. I waved her on.

"We forged a note like the one your mom wrote. And I made sure she knew how to get to the station. I didn't think it would work. But I wanted to help her. Honest to God, Lou, I thought she'd be back by now. I thought for sure they would realize she wasn't you and turn her away."

I pictured Cece at the train station, then on the train. The route was familiar to me only because I'd done it more than once. I knew where I was going. I knew what stops the train made. I knew where the bathrooms were. I knew who would be waiting for me when I got there.

"The problem is, that's as far as we got. She had no plan once she got there. And now I'm scared."

I was scared, too. My mind spun, like it had the day Cece first passed me her note. She could be kidnapped for real this time. Or hurt. Or lost.

The possibilities whirled around my brain and crashed into each other. I needed a way to clear them out. I needed my notebook.

"Lou, what should we do?"

We had to find her.

42

I willed my mind to stop racing.

"We have to find Cece's dad," I said. "We have to tell him where she is."

"I don't want to get her in trouble. Plus, maybe she's not in Kansas City. Maybe she chickened out."

"But what if she is? Don't you think she's in more trouble then?" I didn't give Francie a chance to answer. I stood and walked out of the playground. Francie jogged after me.

"What time was the train?" I asked.

"It left at nine o'clock. She left my house at eight, before anyone else was awake."

"It takes about two and a half hours, so she'd get there around eleven thirty."

I glanced at the time on Mom's phone. 11:12.

"Union Station is big, and it's crowded on the weekends. It would be scary if you don't know where you're going," I said.

Dad always met me at the same spot. I knew where to look the second I stepped off the train. I imagined Cece swept away in the sea of people. Lost. Confused. Alone.

I unlocked Mom's phone. I didn't need her contact list to find the number I wanted. It was another one I knew by heart.

Dad answered on the second ring.

"Hi. Jenny?"

"No. It's me. Lou."

"Lou, baby girl, what's going on?"

"I need your help."

"What's the matter, honey? What's going on?" There was worry in his voice, but it was steady and strong, too.

"Remember the story I said I'd tell you when I see you? It's about that. It's a lot to tell now, so—"

"Tell me what you need."

The river in my ears quieted.

The door to Dad's apartment opened and shut before I was done talking. His feet clomped down the stairs.

"I'm on my way, honey. I won't leave until I find your friend."

~

Mr. Duncan answered the apartment door seconds after we knocked. His phone dangled from his hand, and he wore wrinkled sweatpants and a Missouri Tigers T-shirt with a coffee stain near the sleeve. Opal Duncan sat at the kitchen table holding the Our Lady of Perpetual Help directory.

"Lou! Is Cece with you?" Mr. Duncan looked around me and into the stairwell.

"No. But this is Francie," I said. "And we think we know where Cece is."

He stepped aside and waved us in. We took a few steps forward so we were inside the apartment, but barely.

"Cece's in Kansas City," I said. Francie shifted from one foot to the other.

Mr. Duncan ran a hand through his hair, making it stand on end. He was older and more exhausted every time I saw him. "What? How? Are you sure?"

Opal stood from the table, walked to the door, and placed a hand on Mr. Duncan's shoulder.

"She's in Kansas City," I repeated. "Francie helped her buy the train ticket."

Mr. Duncan ran his hand through his hair again.

"Kansas City? How could that be? Who would let an eleven-year-old on a train alone?" Opal was dressed like she'd come from church, and her face was as stern as ever.

"It's kind of a long story," Francie answered.

And there, in the doorway of the apartment above Able & Payne, we told Mr. Duncan and Opal Duncan everything we knew. I told them about Angel Sweeney. I told them about Cece's plan to come with me to my dad's. And I told them about our fight. Francie told them about the sleepover and their plan. She told them about the tickets and her fears for once Cece got to Kansas City.

Mr. Duncan grew visibly more worried with each piece of information. Even Opal's face seemed to soften, and I read fear there, too.

"We called my dad. He lives in Kansas City, and he's headed to the train station to wait for her," I said. I wanted

Mr. Duncan to know that Cece wasn't in a freefall. That there was someone there to catch her. That she was safe.

But Mr. Duncan seemed frozen, so it was Opal who stepped in and came up with a plan. The first thing she did was call the security office at Union Station in Kansas City.

"Yes, eleven years old. The ticket may have said Louise Bennett, but her name is Cecelia. Cecelia Clark-Duncan... I see... You're sure?"

She pulled the phone away from her face and pushed "end." "They don't think she's there. They said nobody under sixteen can board a train without an adult, and that ticket was never scanned."

Mr. Duncan's eyes filled and he rubbed the tears away.

Francie and I were quiet, and I thought I heard her heart pounding. She inched toward me.

Opal was in take-charge mode. "I'm going to call the Mayfield station. And if she's not there, the police."

Francie reached out and grabbed my hand..

"Eleven years old. Red hair. We didn't see her this morning, but it's almost always in a ponytail... Okay, thank you... We'll be right there."

"Thank God." Mr. Duncan pushed past us. He flew down the stairs two at a time. Opal scurried after him, and Francie and I followed.

43

Mr. Duncan jumped into his car, and Opal climbed into the passenger seat. Before they pulled away, Mr. Duncan stuck his head out the window.

"Do you want to come with us? It might help Cece to see her friends."

I grabbed Francie's hand and pulled her into the back seat. Then the engine revved and the car sped toward Mayfield station at the edge of town.

"Thank you, girls. She's going to be okay." It sounded like he wanted to convince himself as much as he wanted to convince us.

"You did the right thing, girls," Opal added.

Francie gave my hand a squeeze. We rode the rest of the way in silence.

~

The Mayfield station was a small building with a tin roof. A chain-link fence separated it from the tracks. There was nowhere to get lost. Nothing like the sprawling, ornate Union Station.

As soon as the building came into view, so did Cece. She sat on a bench outside. Her sleeping bag and duffel from the sleepover were next to her. Her knees were pulled to her chest, and her head rested on top. Her ponytail was messier than ever.

Cece must've heard the car coming, because as soon as we pulled in, her head popped up. Mr. Duncan had barely put the car in park before he jumped out and flew to her.

Cece ran into his open arms. He bent his head down to whisper something in her ear. Then they stayed like that for a long, long time. Opal got out of the car, but she hung back. I sent Dad a text from Mom's phone, promising to call and explain everything as soon as I could.

When Mr. Duncan and Cece finally broke apart, I creaked the door open and got out of the car. Francie followed. Opal walked toward them, and we followed, keeping our distance.

"So, Mom's in California, huh?" Cece said as we got within earshot.

Mr. Duncan nodded slowly. "But, honey, you have to know it's not about you—"

"She was never going to take me, was she?" Cece's voice cracked and her eyes filled with tears. "I knew it as soon as I got here. I walked into the station, and I was so alone, and I knew it. You, Grandma Opal, Lou. No one was lying to me. But I didn't want to go home. I couldn't. Not after how terrible I'd been. So, I just sat here instead."

I felt the way I had so many times before with Cece. This conversation wasn't meant for me.

"Oh, Cee." Mr. Duncan pulled Cece in tight. "Mom's been struggling—*we've* been struggling. But it has nothing to do with you. Or how much we both love you. Mom is searching for something, and hopefully some time away will help her know what that is. I think she thought a clean break would hurt less. That was wrong of her. I promise the secrets are done now."

Francie reached for my hand again, and this time, I squeezed. A train whistle sounded from somewhere down the track —low and long and lonely. If hurt had a sound, I thought that might be it.

"This isn't the first time she's done this, right? That part wasn't a lie either?"

Now Opal stepped closer. "Cece, I'm sorry. I shouldn't have brought that up. It wasn't my place. I just—"

"I want to know."

"It was a long time ago." Opal looked at Mr. Duncan like she was asking for permission to continue.

He nodded.

"Your father was on a research assignment. Your mother brought you to me and then left town. You were only two years old, and I didn't know where she was or how to get ahold of her. So your father signed that document you found. When she got home, she felt I'd overstepped and overreacted. There were hurt feelings and hurtful words exchanged. On both sides." Opal studied Cece.

Cece tightened her ponytail. "So that's why things were weird between everyone for so long?"

Opal nodded. "It's in the past. And wasn't appropriate for me to bring up in spite. We're all looking for a path forward." She cleared her throat. "And I really hope you'll give me a chance."

Cece nodded, and then she took a deep breath. "I want to talk to her." She wiped her eyes with her fists and jutted out her chin.

Mr. Duncan crouched so he was looking Cece right in the eye. "I will make that happen. I promise."

Then Cece hugged her dad again. Her face was pressed tight against his shirt, so I don't know for sure, but I think she whispered, "I'm sorry."

This time when she pulled back, she seemed to notice me and Francie for the first time. "You came."

"It was kind of the least I could do after I almost got you lost in Kansas City." Francie stared at the ground.

"I'm glad you're okay," I said.

"Me too," Francie said. "I don't know what we were thinking."

"Yeah. Pretty dumb, I guess." Cece used the toe of her black Converse to move a pebble back and forth across the concrete.

"I never even tried to get on the train. I kept thinking about the clues we found—everything Lou figured out." Cece shoved a chunk of hair out of her eye. She hesitated before looking at me. "You were right."

"I didn't want to be right," I said.

"I know."

Our eyes met, and I could tell that she meant it.

Then Cece turned back to her dad and grandmother. "Are you ready to go?"

"Very. Come on, girls. I'll give you a ride home."

Opal got in the front seat next to Mr. Duncan, and Cece, Francie and I piled into the back. Mr. Duncan pulled out onto Eighth Street. He looked at us in the rearview mirror.

"I think this lesson could go without saying, but can you promise me you'll never try something like this again?"

Francie nodded emphatically. "I don't think I've ever been so nervous in my entire life."

"Me either," I said.

Cece stared out the window and didn't say anything. I couldn't tell if she was embarrassed or sad or relieved. Maybe all three.

I directed Mr. Duncan to my house. When he pulled into the driveway, Francie said, "I can get out here, too."

"Are you sure?" Mr. Duncan asked.

"Totally. I've walked home from here about a bazillion times. And plus, I've caused enough trouble. I'm sure you'll be glad to get rid of me."

Mr. Duncan chuckled, but he didn't stop her. I walked toward the house and Francie followed.

"Wait!" Cece rolled down her window. She reached into her duffel bag and pulled out a newspaper. "The new issue of the *Mayfield Gazette*. I grabbed it yesterday, and I had it in my bag. I thought you might want to see it."

"Thanks." I smiled and tucked the paper under my arm.

Cece rolled up her window and Mr. Duncan backed the car out. They drove away.

~

Francie and I stood on my driveway. Neither of us moved to leave.

"Do you think they'll be okay?" Francie asked.

"I don't know, but I hope so."

"So, why did Cece give you a newspaper?"

"For the horoscopes. Angel Sweeney writes them." I opened it to the right page.

Francie moved closer and peeked at the paper over my shoulder.

"They're fun, but just so you know, horoscopes are a watered-down version of real astrology." I repeated Cece's words.

Francie smiled. "Astrology expert now, huh?"

My cheeks flushed. "Cece's the one who—"

"I'm kidding. Your essay was probably so much cooler than mine. Go ahead. I'm interested."

I flipped the paper open and found the Capricorn blurb.

"Release something that's ready to go. An old way of thinking will fall away."

I shivered.

I almost read Francie's for her, but before I could, she did.

"When your spirit feels low, remember you were built to overcome." Francie didn't stumble or stutter once.

That was Cece's horoscope, too. I shivered again.

"I can read, you know. I read it to myself first, so I didn't get tripped up. It's only when I get put on the spot or I'm in front of a lot of people that it's hard."

My chest tightened and the words I wanted to say got stuck.

"I'm not smart like you, Lou, but I'm not dumb, either."

I'm not dumb. It was hard to breathe.

"Francie." It was the only word my throat could squeeze out.

Then Francie pulled her backpack around and unzipped it. "While we're actually talking to each other, I should give you this." Francie pulled out my leather-bound notebook.

A fresh wave of shame washed over me.

"Here." She shook the notebook when I didn't grab it.

"Look, Francie. I—"

I couldn't find the right words to tell her the millions of things I was sorry for.

"I didn't read it, Lou."

She didn't read it? I must've misheard.

"Why would I? It's yours. And besides, I already know what you think about me. I don't need to read it in your notebook." Francie slung her backpack over her shoulder and started to walk away. "I guess I'll see you tomorrow at school." Francie crossed the street and headed toward the Rodriguezes' yard and her shortcut home.

"Francie, wait!" I crossed the street after her.

Francie stopped on the sidewalk and turned around.

Then I said what I should've said fifty-one days ago. I said it without expecting anything from her. There wasn't a plan, or a list, or a script.

There was only the truth.

"Francie, I am so, so sorry. I know I can't unsay words once I've said them, and apologizing will never be enough. But I need you to know how sorry I am."

We stood there for an eternity. If that was the end of the conversation, it would have to be okay. Francie looked right back at me.

"It's fine. You got your true feelings off your chest, I guess."

"It's not fine, and that's not how I feel." But I didn't know how to make her believe that. I had hurled words into the space between us before.

At least I know how to read...

Maybe if your mom cared about you a little more...

How was Francie supposed to know that those words weren't true, but these words were?

"You're the smartest person I know. I've always thought that."

"You don't have to say that. I get it. You're sorry you embarrassed me. And like I said, it's fine. Anyway, I never should've texted Braden. He's a jerk."

"Francie." I fought the urge to count backward. "I don't know why I said any of it. I was mad about Braden and scared you were going to choose Tommy over me. I thought you were going to figure out you never should've chosen me in the first place."

"Chosen you? Seriously?" Francie laughed to herself. "I always thought you were the one who chose me."

"Then you were wrong. Don't you remember the first day of school in Sister Mary Joseph's kindergarten class?"

A smile played at the corners of Francie's mouth. "I

guess that explains everything. Back then I still ate glue and couldn't figure out how to sit criss-cross applesauce."

We both laughed, and a burst of joy shot through my chest. I tried grabbing onto it, but as quickly as it came, it went. Francie walked away.

"Wait. There's one more thing." I took a deep breath. "That thing I said about your mom."

Francie froze.

"Everything with Cece made me see that it wasn't just the stuff I said, it's—I hadn't been a good friend before that either. And I'm so sorry." I gripped the notebook in my hands until my knuckles turned white, and Francie turned to face me.

"I know you are," she whispered.

But I wasn't sure if she did know. Or what else I should say.

Francie turned back around. She took a few steps, and then she stopped and turned back to me. "Maybe you didn't mean it, but it really hurt, you know?"

"I know," I said.

"I couldn't believe the one person I thought never would, could hurt me like that."

My eyes filled with tears. "I know."

"But I messed up a lot, too. I should've listened to you, and I should've been a better friend. I know I haven't acted like it, but being your best friend always made me feel so lucky," Francie said.

I didn't say it out loud, but now I knew that, too.

Where would we go from there? The words I'd said would always exist between us, and I didn't think Francie would forget them. And the truth was Francie had hurt me, too. We were both changing, and the only thing I knew for sure was that we couldn't go backward.

"But I've missed you, Lou. I mean that and I'm tired of being mad. I'll see you tomorrow, okay?" Francie turned to go.

I sucked in a breath. "See you tomorrow."

And then she walked away.

I blinked back my tears and tried to breathe through the lump in my throat. Maybe it would be okay. Maybe she did forgive me. And maybe I forgave her, too.

TWO DAYS BEFORE SIXTH GRADE

Francie spent the night at my house two nights before school started. It was our tradition. The next night—the night before the first day—was an official "school night." So we did everything we could to make that last night special. The Last Night of Summer.

James made us homemade pizzas with our favorite toppings. Pepperoni and mushrooms for me. Ham and pineapple for Francie. Mom let us stay up watching movies as late as we wanted. Sometimes we rode bikes and spied in the neighborhood before dinner.

On the Last Night of Summer before sixth grade, Francie had a different idea.

"Remember those time capsules we made at the end of third grade in Sister Genevieve's class?"

Mine was tucked away in the back of my closet. I hadn't thought about it in a long time, but I planned to follow Sister

Genevieve's directions and open it when we graduated from Our Lady of Perpetual Help in eighth grade.

"Tess made one this year, but she couldn't wait. She opened it and showed it to me and Bernie this morning," Francie said.

"That sounds like her," I said. "Mine's still in my closet."

"I'm pretty sure mine got thrown away with a bunch of my other school stuff. What if we made new ones?"

"Tonight?" I didn't hate this idea. It was a million times better than analyzing Francie's latest conversation with Tommy at the pool snack bar or talking about how to style the school uniform to make sure we looked "cute" on the first day.

"Yeah. Like a friendship capsule. We can open it when we graduate from high school. Or maybe when we're old ladies with white hair, drinking coffee on the porch and talking about 'the good old days.'" Francie laughed.

"I love it," I said. I'd never meant anything more.

We found an empty shoebox in Mom's closet and set to work filling it and telling stories as we went.

A medal from the soccer team we both quit in second grade after Francie realized she'd get benched every time she pushed someone to the ground when they stole the ball from her. A picture of us at Six Flags in fourth grade. We rode the Screamin' Eagle so many times we were both dizzy for a week. A note passed during class in fifth grade. We passed so many notes, Sister Rosemary assigned us permanent seats in opposite corners of the room.

Tears streamed down my face from laughing too hard.

Francie rolled onto my bed. "Oh my God, Lou. Stop. My stomach hurts!"

My heart burst wide open, and for that night, Francie stopped walking away. I was next to her. She was right there.

"Do you still have that paper from the first night we did the spying game?" Francie pulled the shoebox into her lap.

"Yeah, I do." I had tucked it into the back of my sock drawer the night of the fish fry. I felt it every now and then when I was digging around for a sock's match, but I'd never thrown it away.

"Let's put that in there, then. And maybe one of your old notebooks. That game was so us, *you know?"*

My heart caught on was.

"I love us, *don't you?" Francie grinned.*

And just like that, my heart soared again.

The first thing I did when I got home was call Dad. He said he'd figured out pretty quickly that Cece had never made it to Kansas City.

"I hope things work out for your friend," he said.

"Me too."

"And, hey, Loulie. Thanks for calling me. You call me any time you need me. Got it?"

"Got it." I wished I could reach through the phone and squeeze him so that his beard scratched my face. The way I did when I was little.

"And, I was thinking, about our weekend together. What if I come to Mayfield instead? I could get a hotel room, and you could do all that Halloween stuff. But if you hate that idea—"

"I love it."

~

Cece wasn't at school most of the next week, but I watched the door for her messy red ponytail and black Converse sneakers every morning.

So much had happened that I hardly even worried about my notebook. I had it back, and that was what mattered. Of course, Braden was the one who couldn't let it go.

"Hey Lou, I never got a chance to finish reading your secret diary. What'd you have to say about me?"

"Absolutely nothing, Braden. You've never been worth my time." It was true and saying so made my chest swell. What he said didn't matter.

Francie was at her desk, but she turned around when she heard me. She gave me a giant smile and a thumbs-up.

I was still a colt learning to walk on shaky legs around her. It was hard to know where I belonged. Or if I belonged at all. There were glimmers of the Old Francie, though.

She saved me a seat at lunch. And at recess, when I wandered toward the spot by the fence, she called out to me.

"Lou! Where are you going? Come sit with us." She was under the rusty slide. So were Madison and Annabelle.

But the New Francie was there, too.

Her mascara was thick, her skirt was rolled, and she passed notes with Tommy throughout math class on Tuesday.

I prayed that someday things wouldn't be so hard. That we would fit together as easily as we once had. I couldn't know for sure if that would happen. But I didn't let myself get stuck counting backward. I forced my wobbly legs to keep stepping forward, even when they stepped toward Francie and away from her at the same time.

~

On Wednesday after school, as I walked up our driveway, I spotted something sitting squarely in the middle of the welcome mat. I got closer, and it was a note folded into the shape of an origami frog.

Lou was written across the front.

I pulled the tongue to open it, and a second sheet of paper fluttered onto the porch. The paper had the Scorpio constellation across the top. A letter. From Cece's notebook. This is what it said:

Dear Lou,

I'm so sorry for everything, but especially the notebook. I was mad and hurt. I know that's not a great excuse, and if you hate me, I understand. But I really hope you don't.

I wanted to say more at the station, but I just couldn't. Sometimes words are easier when they're written. So, here goes.

As soon as we got to Mayfield, it was like Mercury in retrograde. Things were mixed up and backward, and I was getting it all wrong.

When I was waiting at the station, I had this memory. I was five and my parents took me to the Missouri State Fair. I loved it. But then we were walking to the Tilt-A-Whirl and suddenly every adult standing around me was a stranger. I'd drifted away from my parents.

The ending to the story that I'd always remembered was that my mom burst through the crowd and found me.

Ever since we got to Mayfield, I wanted my mom to burst in again and find me. I even hoped she'd be at the station that day.

But deep down I knew she wouldn't. And I had no idea what I was doing there.

And as I sat there it hit me. I was remembering it wrong. My dad was the one who found me at the fair, and he found me at the station, too. Just like I knew, deep down, he would.

I've been wrong about so much.

I hope you read all of this. And I hope you know I'm really sorry.

CCD

PS: My mom is going to call me tomorrow. I'm nervous, and mad, too. Do you think you could be there with me when she calls? If the answer is yes, meet me after school tomorrow. If the answer is no, you can pretend I never asked.

~

The presentation for the Christ Is Alive! essay contest was the next day.

The entire sixth grade filed into the front row of the auditorium. Our family members filled the seats behind us. I turned around in my seat to get a good look at who was there.

I spotted Mom and James immediately. They sat toward the middle, and it looked like they were holding hands over the arm rest.

In the corner, sitting a few rows away from everyone else, I spotted Francie's parents. Both of them. Mrs. Fitzpatrick fiddled with a string of rosary beads she had wrapped around her wrist. She seemed nervous. But she was there.

Francie sat at the end of the row, and I could tell she saw them, too. A smile kept sneaking across her face.

As the lights dimmed and Dr. Morgan took the stage to welcome the guests, the auditorium doors swung open. I saw the outline of her messy ponytail before she stepped into the light. Cece was back, and Mr. Duncan was right behind her. She started toward our row. Then she stopped and turned back. She gave her dad a hug. He nudged her forward, and she took the last empty seat, two down from me.

Dr. Morgan stood behind the podium.

"Welcome sixth graders, parents, and guests. We are honored to have with us today some distinguished and Christlike members of our community..."

"Lou! Pssst! Lou!" Francie leaned forward in her seat. She pointed to a small piece of paper in her hand. Then in the same not-so-quiet whisper, "It's for Cece."

Francie slid the paper across the floor. It stopped when it hit my white sneaker. I didn't pick it up, but I could see what she wrote from my seat. A smiley face and under that: *Welcome back, Cece!!*

I pushed it toward Cece with my toe. Then I reached across Annabelle, who sat next to me, and tapped Cece's knee to let her know it was there. It took me a moment to realize Francie's note didn't make me scared, or angry, or jealous. I wanted Cece to know she had a place here, and I was glad Francie wanted to give her that, too. There was plenty of room for all of us.

And Francie's note gave me an idea. I tore out a page from my notebook.

I'll be there for the phone call. Meet me in front of the buses after school. Lou

I slid it across the floor to Cece. Her face brightened as she read it.

It had been four whole days since I'd needed to count backward. I knew I wasn't done with that forever, but I was okay. And time would keep moving forward.

I was ready to move forward, too.

THE 141ST DAY OF SIXTH GRADE

My twelfth birthday was our first day back at school after Winter Break—January 6. Coming back to school after a long break is always hard. Everything is familiar and strange at the same time.

James dropped me off at school that morning because it was too cold to walk, and Mom was busy with my siblings. I was the first one in the classroom, which only ever happens when James is my ride. I wasn't alone long, though, before the buses got to school and everyone started streaming in.

Cece burst in while I was hanging up my coat.

"Lou! Hi!" She'd replaced her messy ponytail with a topknot, still messy, but different enough to give me that strange/familiar feeling.

Cece was the only friend I'd seen over the break. We'd taken the train to Kansas City together two days after Christmas. I spent a week with Dad, and she spent a few days with her mom. Cece's mom had come to Mayfield after she got back from San Francisco in November. She stayed for a few days and then went to Kansas City, where she had rented an apartment downtown. The trip was Cece's first time seeing it. I knew Cece wanted her parents to work things out, but on the train, we'd talked about what would happen if they didn't.

She was going to be okay. I knew that. And she did, too.

"How was Kansas City?" I asked.

"Better than I thought it would be. But there was a significant planet alignment, so that's probably why."

I smiled. This Cece was familiar/familiar.

"I promise, I'll tell you everything later. But it's your birthday! So we should manifest positive energy to you right now." Cece reached into her messenger bag and pulled out a paper sack dotted with grease stains.

"Nettie's?" I asked.

Cece handed me the bag and I peered inside. A Nettie's chocolate Long John stared up at me. "You are the best!"

"Did you get enough to share?" Francie swooped into the coatroom and looked over Cece's shoulder into the Nettie's bag. "Happy birthday, Lou! Your last one as a kid. Next year, we'll be teenagers—how cool is that?"

I tried not to think about that. But, of course Francie would think becoming a teenager was cool and not completely terrifying. Things were good between us, though. Not perfect, but good. And I understood that it had never been perfect. There's no such thing.

"I'm just going to focus on being twelve for now," I said.

"I brought you something, too." Francie held out a rectangular package wrapped in pink tissue. The corners of the paper were folded and carefully taped, and the tissue paper was bright like bubble gum. I was pretty sure I knew what was inside, but Francie had never wrapped my birthday present before. Strange/familiar.

Francie gave me the package, and I handed her the Nettie's bag. She popped a bite of donut into her mouth, but I held the gift close to my chest, not wanting to rip into it.

"Are you going to open it or what?" Francie said.

I peeled back the taped corners, trying not to tear the paper. I slipped the gift out, and the tissue fluttered to the floor.

"A notebook! I thought we were done with these."

Francie shrugged. "You needed a place to start fresh. And besides, it's our tradition. You wouldn't be Lou without your notebook."

Before, the notebook thing had always felt like ours. Francie didn't have to come right out and say it, but I knew this notebook was mine. I felt a twinge of sadness about that, but it didn't threaten to swallow me whole. And just as gently as it came, it went. I smiled at Francie.

"Thank you. This means a lot to me." And I meant it.

"The bell is going to ring in two minutes." Mrs. Jackson's voice cut through into the coatroom. "Let's start the new year right by finding our seats and getting started on our morning work. There's a journal prompt on the board."

I picked the pink tissue paper off the ground and stuffed it into the trash can as I followed Francie and Cece into the classroom. Excited chatter died down as everyone found their desks and followed Mrs. Jackson's directions.

I placed the notebook in the corner of my desk and ran my fingers over the buttery cover. I didn't even have to bend my head down to breathe in the new leather smell.

I pulled out my school journal and read the prompt Mrs. Jackson had on the board: "Sometimes the best way to move forward is to take a look back. What are some truths from the past year that will help you in the year ahead?"

I turned around in my seat. Cece's pencil was already furiously scratching across her page. She stopped to push a loose piece of hair back toward her topknot and kept going. Across the room, Francie rested her head in her hand while the other hand moved in a circular pattern. She was drawing spirals. Familiar/familiar.

I started to write in my journal, and then I changed my mind. I shoved the journal in my desk, pulled my new leather notebook in front of me, and opened to the first page.

Truths to Carry with Me

1. It's okay to feel stuck, to even want to go backward, as long as you eventually figure out how to keep moving forward.

2. People sometimes get hurt and sometimes do the hurting, but an apology goes a long way.

3. Even when you really, really want to hold on, sometimes you have to let go.

What I wrote sounded like one of Angel's horoscopes, but the words were true, so I left them. I stopped writing and glanced over at Francie. Tommy leaned across his desk toward her chair and she tipped her head back so she could hear whatever he was saying. Francie laughed, and then kicked Madison's chair to get her attention.

I turned around to see if Cece was still writing. She put her pencil down and looked up. She smiled at me and waved. I waved back.

I turned back to my list and added a line to number three.

3. Even when you really, really want to hold on, sometimes you have to let go—so you don't miss out on what's coming next.

I underlined the last part three times. Then I closed my notebook.

ACKNOWLEDGMENTS

I've wanted to be an author since I learned how to read, so seeing this story become a book has been one of the greatest joys of my life. I have so many people to thank for that.

To Sally Morgridge, my editor, for helping me find the very best version of this story. And to the team at Holiday House: Mary Cash, Laura Kincaid, Raina Putter, Rebecca Godan, Amy Toth, and the entire marketing/publicity department, my deepest thanks for all the work that went into making this dream a reality.

To Elizabeth Bennett, my incredible agent. Thank you for believing in this story and in me. Your support means the world.

To Ramona Kaulitzki for creating the gorgeous cover. It's perfect.

To Megan E. Freeman and Nicole M. Hewitt, my mentors through Author Mentor Match. You helped me find the story I was trying to tell, and this story wouldn't be a book without your thoughtful and thorough feedback. Thank you.

To Lisa Daly, Barb Hopkins, and Sarah Mohler, my brilliant and kind critique partners. Your honest feedback and unwavering support were exactly what I needed to believe this was a dream worth pursuing.

To my writing group, the Middle Grade Waves, especially those who read different versions and pieces of this book. I'm grateful to have you in my corner.

To my closest friends and family for seeing me as a writer. I am so lucky.

To Pam and Gary Burgard, my parents, who have believed wholeheartedly in every dream I've ever had (even Olympic-sized ones). Every kid deserves that, but I was lucky enough to get it. I hope I can do the same for my own kids.

To Andy, my husband, whose confidence and optimism gave me the courage to actually sit down and write. You believed this story would be a book even when I didn't (and before you even read it). What an incredible gift.

And to Will, Jack, Claire, and Kate, my smart, funny, creative, and kind children. You are the greatest joy of my life. I love you.